Table of Contents

Chapter One 7

Chapter Two 16

Chapter Three................................ 25

Chapter Four 33

Chapter Five 42

Chapter Six 48

Chapter Seven 56

Chapter Eight 67

Chapter Nine 75

Chapter Ten.................................81

Chapter Eleven 88

Chapter Twelve................................ 95

Chapter Thirteen 102

Chapter Fourteen 108

Chapter Fifteen................................ 117

Chapter Sixteen 125

Chapter Seventeen 139

Chapter Eighteen 152

Chapter Nineteen 161

Chapter Twenty 175

Chapter Twenty-one 185

Chapter Twenty-two 194

Chapter Twenty-three 208

Chapter Twenty-Four 241

The New World

Climate of Fire, Book Three
Shirley Bigelow DeKelver

Print ISBNs
Amazon print 9780228638858
Ingram Spark 9780228638865
Barnes & Noble 9780228638872
BWL Print 9780228638889

[BWL Publishing Logo with business name and url]

Dedication

For my husband Butch,
whose love and patience
provided me with support and
encouragement I needed to
complete Book Three of my trilogy.

Acknowledgements

BWL Publishing acknowledges the Government of Canada and the Canada Book Fund for its financial support in creating the Canadian Historical Mysteries collection.

Funded by the Government of Canada | **Canada**

[Government of Canada Logo]

BWL Publishing acknowledges the Province of Alberta for their ongoing support through the Alberta Publishers Cultural Industry Operating Grant.

Alberta Government

[Government of Alberta logo]

[Certified Canadian Publisher Badge]

Author Acknowledgement

To my immediate and extended families, always willing to listen to me, encourage me, and love me unconditionally. To my friends and members of The Shuswap Association of Writers, Word on the Lake Writers Festival, Writers Nook, and the Shuswap Writers Group, who provided positive reinforcement in helping me reach my goals.

Chapter One

My two best friends, Taylor and Mai-Li have betrayed me. Taylor professed his love to me, announced he wanted to marry me and provide a home for Eddie, but first I must absolve Willie. Shocked, I angrily rejected his ultimatum, I could never forgive Willie. I ran from Taylor and hid in our house, denying myself food and refusing access to anyone who knocked on the door.

Days later, Mai-Li arrived, along with her bodyguards, and insisted I allow her to enter. She commanded I pardon Willie, if I repudiated, none of us would find peace. I understood I would lose both her friendship and Taylor's love when I defied her order. Mai-Li's parting words would remain with me the rest of my life. *"I cannot allow you to remain in Blackfoot, we have no room for resentment and malevolence, you must leave."*

When I enquired if Taylor and Eddie must go as well, she told me Taylor left days before with Chief Johnson. Kim Lee was taking care of Eddie while he was gone.

I made appeals to meet with Mai-Li and sought her permission to see Eddie; however, she declined my requests. A week passed and the day before I left, she agreed to let me say goodbye. Leaving him was crushing and one of the toughest decisions I ever made. I promised him, amid his tears and pleas, that I would do everything possible to return.

Taylor's unexpected departure left me stunned, and I grappled with feelings of abandonment and self-doubt. There was no place for me in Blackfoot.

My thoughts returned to the present. I stared at Lance's back, he wore his black hair in a long braid, had almond-shaped eyes, a straight nose, and a full mouth. His body was muscular, and he wore a buckskin jacket, leggings, and moccasins. He carried a bow and a quiver of arrows.

Since we left Blackfoot, I seldom spoke and answered only when questioned. Lance was quiet by nature and accepted my sullenness.

We rode due north, following the Similkameen River. We did not travel far, as it was late in the afternoon when we started our journey.

He stopped and dismounted. "It's turning dark," he announced, as he reached and took my horse's reins. "Let's find a place to camp, and then you should share your plans with me."

I grabbed the saddle horn and stiffly flung my leg over my horse's back. He neighed, stepped back, and spun around. Lance grunted and at once settled him, then helped me dismount. It was clear how uncomfortable and nervous I was around horses.

I tailed Lance and the horses down a narrow footpath and arrived at a flat clearing. He asked if I brought a tent or a tarp, and my face turned red with embarrassment. I shook my head and stared at the ground. In my haste to leave, I forgot to pack the small tent. I searched for the tarp but could not find it, and assumed Taylor took it with him when he left with Chief Johnson.

"I have a knife," I offered, hoping to make amends. "I hide it in my boot."

"Thank you," Lance smiled. "I have rope, and an axe. There is no better time than now to teach you how to build a lean-to."

He put me to work collecting wood, pine needles, and boughs, and instructed me to find three long pieces of wood. He pointed to two nearby cedars and showed me how to make a domed frame to lean against their trunks, stressing the entrance must face out of the wind. Then he instructed me to tie thin pieces of wood to the frame as support beams for a roof. My head was spinning as I followed his instructions. It was not long when we finished building the shelter and I helped him remove our supplies and backpacks from the horses and set them inside.

Lance unsaddled the horses, while I watched closely. "What are the horses' names?"

"You're riding Thunder, and I'm riding Ginger, she's cantankerous at times, then, again, most females are."

"Hey," I exclaimed. Lance chuckled, then turned and faced me. "Tomorrow, you can harness your own horse, and I'll show you how to groom and water Thunder."

I nodded. "I will gather firewood and start a fire. That I know how to do."

When I had packed this morning, I discovered the fridge and cupboards were almost empty. I made sandwiches with the leftovers, then found a bag of plums and half a box of crackers, which I stuffed in a cloth bag I found in the closet. There was enough food to last me three days at the most; now that Lance joined me, I realized there was enough for one day, then we would have to rely on trapping small game animals and picking plants and herbs.

I handed two sandwiches to Lance and took one for myself. "How much food do we have left?"

"A couple of sandwiches, some plums, and half a bag of crackers, maybe enough until tomorrow," I answered.

"You know how to hunt?"

"When we lived at the cabin, I hunted with Taylor. Mai-Li did all the cooking and watched the kids."

He raised his eyebrows in surprise. I imagine the idea of Mai-Li, leader of the Chinese people cooking for six people and minding two young children, was complicated to grasp.

"Taylor hunted with his bow and arrow. He tried to teach me how to use them, unfortunately I was a hopeless case. I didn't have enough strength in my arms and shoulder muscles. That's when he decided to teach me how to fire a gun, we used blanks because our ammunition supply was low."

Lance watched me as I turned and stared moodily at the fire, captivated by the crackling and snapping sounds of the sparks. I finished my sandwich, then wrapped my arms tightly around my waist. "The lessons stopped when we left the cabin unexpectedly."

"Can I ask what happened?"

"Willie happened," I answered. "If you don't mind, I'd rather not discuss it."

Lance nodded, not pursuing the matter. "Taylor told us about your travels and how you struggled to survive, and your amazing fortune in finding the cabin. I am sorry about the little boy who died."

I jerked and raised my head sharply. "That's over and done with," I expressed harshly. "And so is Taylor."

Lance said nothing, and I tossed a plum pit into the bushes. The silence was deafening; I raised my head, then cleared my throat. "You told me your grandfather requested you make sure I arrive safely at my destination, yet he and Taylor left days ago, how could he know I would be summoned to leave?"

"When he bade you to meet with him, it was your response when he informed you Willie would remain in Blackfoot, and he hoped you would exonerate him. He must have spoken to Taylor, who mentioned he had discussed the matter with you as well and received the same comeback. My grandfather is extremely insightful, and he knew Mai-Li would not have allowed you to remain in Blackfoot under those circumstances."

"Which obviously made it easier for Taylor to leave without informing me."

Lance remained silent, and I soon regretted airing my anger and bitterness with a stranger. I exhaled, then turned and faced him. "I'm sorry, I didn't mean to dump that on you."

"And I shouldn't have been so nosy. How about we return to our earlier discussion, have you chosen a destination yet?"

"I haven't given it much thought," I shrugged. "I was summoned to leave quite suddenly."

Lance lowered his head and waited for me to speak.

"I don't know this part of BC at all. I grew up in Vancouver, and after the earthquake and tsunami, I took shelter on Little Mountain and lived on my own for almost two years. Then I met Rusty and Eddie, and we found an old warehouse where we stayed for a while. We were barely surviving when Willie came into our lives. I made the disastrous decision to let him join our group, only because he knew where to find hidden caches of food. Mai-Li and Debbie joined us later, and I met Taylor when I was foraging, and we both took cover in a sewer pipe during a violent thunderstorm."

"How did he end up with your group?"

"When I got back to the warehouse, the place was in an uproar. I knew Mai-Li and the kids were worried about me when I didn't come home the night before, which was why the boys were acting up. As usual, Willie sat and watched without offering to help. I was so angry I tore a strip off him; he would have retaliated, except Mai-Li interfered. He was at the receiving end once when Mai-Li used her martial arts to stop him from bullying Debbie, which is why he backed off. The next day we took the kids to a park, and Willie tracked us. He was still upset with me, and got mean, and stole my knife. He was going to use it on me when Taylor intruded and stopped him. That's how Taylor came into our lives."

"Why did you guys decide to leave Little Mountain?"

"At first, it was a God send, it was located on the highest point in West Vancouver and protected us from the tsunami. As time passed, food became scarce, and the gangs were becoming more violent. It was Taylor who suggested we go to the Interior, and if we weren't successful, we would head north. That was when Mai-Li offered us a home in Blackfoot."

"Do you mind if I ask what happened between you and Willie?"

I lifted my head and stared into the darkness. "He kidnapped me and physically abused me. I cannot exonerate him for what he did, and I cannot forgive Taylor and Mai-Li taking his side. Your grandfather's decision to let Willie stay in Blackfoot was the reason I had to leave and why I lost Eddie."

Lance looked at me. "Thanks for telling me about Willie, and I am sorry this happened to you, I have no respect for a man who abuses a woman."

"Those are just words, Lance, they cannot erase what I endured. That is why I must find a place where I can start again and find someone who will care for me. Know one thing, when the time is right, I will return for Eddie."

Then I stood, entered the lean-to, and crawled inside my sleeping bag. It took me some time to fall asleep. My mind returned to my last encounter with Taylor, and what we discussed. He did not let me know he was going with Chief Johnson, or for that matter when he would return. I'm sure he assumed I would be requested to leave Blackfoot and chose not to discuss it with me in advance.

Then why did it hurt so much?

Chapter Two

I woke with a jolt when I heard movement outside the lean-to. I rose and stumbled outside.

"Morning," I murmured.

Lance was sitting on his sleeping bag. He nodded and threw a log into the coals, then poked the ashes with a long stick. "You did not rest well last night; I heard you tossing."

I sat on the ground and shivered. I zipped my jacket and warmed my hands over the embers. The morning air was chilly and damp while creeping wisps of mist covered the underbrush and wrapped around the trunks of the trees.

"I was thinking about what we talked about yesterday."

"You suffered both emotional and physical abuse, which is a horrific burden to live with. Don't let it consume you, give yourself time, and eventually you will come to terms with it."

"Taylor told me the same when he..." I stopped in mid-sentence. Lance raised his head and looked at me, sensing my discomfort.

I overheard the horses as they moved in the bushes and recognized Thunder's dark outline. He raised his head and nickered softly.

"He greets you," Lance explained. "He has taken a liking to you, as a rule he is more selective."

"Yes, males are like that," I mumbled.

He chuckled softly, which surprised me as I got the impression it was rare for him to joke around.

"Let's return to more important issues, have you given any consideration about your destination?"

"I'm sorry I didn't answer earlier because I have no idea what I wish to do or where I want to go. I considered moving to Princeton, I might find work there, in the art field."

"I know you are a talented artist; however, it's a competitive field, and I believe you do not have the experience or training necessary. Do you have skills in other areas?"

"No, not really. I was sixteen when the earthquake hit Vancouver. Since then, I was homeless, and this past year our group spent time travelling to the Interior."

"How old are you, Carlie?"

"Eighteen, I'll be nineteen in August."

"Unfortunately, what I can gather from what you told me, the young adults who survived the earthquake endured on their own and struggled to stay alive. It will be a long time before they find their roots. As for Princeton, it is an unforgiving place. It would not be safe for any woman to try to exist there on her own. I appreciate you struggled to reach the Interior, nonetheless you were with people who protected you and helped you to survive."

"You're referring to Taylor and Mai-Li, and I suppose Willie?"

Lance nodded. "Not what you care to hear, but yes."

"I appreciate your insight regarding Princeton; however, I would prefer to survive on my own in the wilderness than return to Blackfoot and face Willie again. I am not willing to exonerate him, and I don't know if I ever will."

"That is understandable, you must do what your heart tells you."

I shuffled uncomfortably; aware Lance was not expecting a response.

"Have you considered returning to the cabin," he mentioned.

"I did, although from what you've just told me," I answered as I raised my voice in frustration. "How would that be any different than trying to make it on my own in Princeton?"

"I appreciate your irritation; can I suggest an alternative. I know settlers in the area who might be willing to take you in, some of them have infants and young children and are building cabins and putting in gardens and could use an extra hand."

"It's not that I don't appreciate your suggestion, Lance, except I don't believe I would be content living with strangers, it's critical I find a new purpose in my life."

Lance nodded and waited for me to proceed.

"I'm not helpless, I know how to hunt small game animals, grouse, quail and rabbits, and Taylor showed me how to trap fish. I wouldn't be able to hunt deer or moose, I don't have the strength or the weapons to do that, and I learned a lot from Mai-Li about herbs and edible plants, I just wish I'd paid closer attention to the preparation and cooking part."

We sat in silence; I gathered what I just shared with him was not enough to convince him I could make it on my own.

"I can protect myself," I whispered. "During our travels, we had an altercation with one of the gangs in the Wastelands. I killed a man."

Lance straightened his back, drew his lips back, and widened his eyes in surprise.

"We sought shelter for the night in a train car and were attacked. We defended ourselves as best we could, I was supporting Rusty and Eddie in my arms, and Mai-Li was protecting Debbie. One of the gang members climbed into the sidecar through a back window, he aimed his gun directly at me. I threw my knife at him and killed him the same time he fired his gun. The bullet hit

Rusty, and he died in my arms. He was only ten years old."

"I am sorry you were forced to relive that memory," Lance replied. "When Rusty died, you took on the sole care of Eddie, and I understand why you cannot accept Mai-Li's decision he remain with her."

"I tried to convince her Eddie needed to be with me; she refused to change her mind. I saw how our dispute affected him; it wasn't fair to put him in the middle. I accepted her request because for now, it's the best solution. In time, when I'm able, I will go back for him."

"If that is what your heart tells you, then you will be reunited with him."

I listened to the calming and predictable sound of chirping birds and rustling leaves and branches.

"One other thing, before anything can be settled," Lance exclaimed. "Have you finally decided where you want to go?"

"Yes, I'm going back to the cabin," I announced.

"I am not surprised. I will accompany you, travelling by horseback is speedier and safer and I do not believe you should attempt to hike there on your own."

"Lance, I cannot let you do that, you will be expected back in Blackfoot, with your grandfather absent, you must have responsibilities and duties."

"When he left, Grandfather requested I go with you to your chosen destination. I am a man, and my decisions are my own."

"How will your family know where you are?" I asked casually.

"I'll get word back to them," he responded.

Trying to keep a straight face I said. "I suppose you could always send a smoke signal?"

The look on Lance's face was hilarious. "Not a wise decision, with the widespread wildfires we encounter. I'll leave a note attached to one of the trees along the trail. The next person who passes this way will take it with them."

I nodded in agreement.

"You obviously watched too much television growing up," he said, as he cleared his throat, his eyes glittering with laughter. "My people stopped sending smoke signals years ago."

I snorted and realized this was one argument I was not about to win.

"Then why don't you have a mobile phone; I know Blackfoot has electricity," I inquired. "Wouldn't that be safer and easier?"

"Our town has a limited power source, which is intended for necessities like lighting, refrigeration, heating, and cooling systems in the houses, schools, and buildings. There's a central laundry that all residents have access to. If you wish to converse with someone, you go to their homes or attend the gatherings at the Community Hall."

"Growing up in Vancouver was significantly different," I added. "The power usage was staggering. Numerous families owned or rented residences complete with appliances, sometimes two televisions, mobile phones, and computers."

"Carlie, hopefully when Vancouver is rebuilt, people will address these issues and start over," Lance whispered.

"As the residents of Blackfoot did?"

"A conversation we can discuss later," Lance mentioned. "I've decided to ride back to Blackfoot, you mentioned you left your small tent behind, I'll pick it up. I have a tarp, and I want to acquire extra supplies as well. I do not intend to make a lean-to every time we stop. Do you have a flashlight or a propane lantern?"

I shook my head. "Taylor owned a flashlight, and so did Mai-Li. Finding batteries was always a problem, so we used them sparingly. Taylor didn't care for gas lanterns as he worried about fires."

"That makes sense. Anything to add to your list?"

I shook my head. "I can't think of anything, should I go back with you?"

"I can make better time on my own riding Ginger; while I'm gone, fetch water from the river and boil it, then fill your water container. We'll need food, I recall you telling me you've hunted small game?"

I nodded.

"See if you can find something, and don't stray too far."

"Take the rest of the sandwiches with you, I'll make do with the plums and crackers," I suggested.

Lance whistled, and Ginger trotted towards him. He leapt on her back without saddling or haltering her.

"How long will you be gone?" I inquired.

"Not more than two or three hours, take your rifle with you when you go to the river or into the bush. Stay alert, there's been bears spotted in the area."

"Don' forget to tell someone you'll be going with me to the cabin," I reminded.

"I imagine they'll figure that out when I come back for a tent, a tarp and supplies."

"Just saving you from having to write a note and nailing it to a tree."

He grunted, stuffed a sandwich in his mouth, and steered Ginger towards the path. I watched as the spirited horse galloped over a knoll and disappeared.

I mulled over the shift in plans; grateful I did not have to travel to the cabin on my own; and travelling by horseback would cut hours from my journey. Lance was well versed in wilderness survival, and his company and sense of humour were a bonus.

I sensed I made the right decision; I was going home!

One day I would disclose to Lance that Willie was the leader of the gang in Little Mountain who attacked Rusty and Eddie, and that he was a bully and a coward.

Chapter Three

The first thing I did was hike to the river. I filled the container and returned to our camping spot, poured water into the metal pot, and placed it over the flames. I decided to air the sleeping bags and tossed them over a bush.

The sun poked its way through the clouds, and I welcomed its warm embrace. I added wood to the campfire and decided to clean my backpack. I left Blackfoot in such a hurry, I had crammed everything inside without checking to see if I had packed everything I needed.

I dumped the entire contents on the ground when unexpectedly I was overcome with grief. I burst into tears, stirring memories of Eddie on our journey to the Interior, and the difficulty he always had strapping on his backpack. I would chuckle when he shyly pleaded for help. Leaving Eddie behind with Mai-Li distressed me as much as when Rusty died in my arms. I did not know what to expect in the future, but I realized how important it was to put Taylor out of my mind and try to forget how much he hurt me. Rusty would forever remain in my heart; when the time was favourable, I would return for Eddie.

I wiped my tears with the back of my hand, then repacked my clothing and personal items. I heard Thunder moving in the bush, and I strolled into the trees and approached him. I patted his muzzle and scratched his forelock. He pushed his muzzle against my hand, enjoying the attention,

"You like being spoiled, don't you?" I whispered. He playfully nipped my fingers, and I left him to graze. I returned to the fire, removed the pot, and set it aside to cool. It would be a while until Lance returned. I doused the flames with the unused water in the container, carefully checked the embers were out and retrieved my rifle and ammunition case. I reached down and felt my knife in its casing.

I hiked into the brush and discovered an animal trail leading to the forest. I always enjoyed late May, the pleasant weather and the scent of wildflowers. I passed massive oaks, fir trees, and gigantic ponderosa pines.

I picked up my pace, then without warming I overheard a shuffle in the undergrowth. I froze and raised my rifle and remembered to release the trigger guard. A ruffled beating of wings startled me, and I spotted a ruffed grouse flying directly towards me. Before it could escape and take safety in a nearby cover, I fired. It dropped heavily to the ground.

I returned to camp and spent the next half hour removing its feathers and innards (a chore I detested). When I was through, I put the cleaned carcass inside the lean-to. I poured cool water into the container and re-lit the fire.

As Lance predicted, it was not long before he returned, gripping the reins of a second horse carrying supplies. He waved and jumped nimbly to the ground.

"You made excellent time, were there any problems?"

"No fussbudget," he said. "I found your tent, and after gathering the rest of our supplies, I decided to bring a packhorse. The trails ahead of us are quite steep, no sense tiring our mounts."

"He's beautiful," I declared, as I stroked his withers. "What's his name?"

"Ringo. He's part Morgan, regrettably, he hates being ridden. I spent time trying to tame him; however, he has a mind of his own. Don't stand too close, he bites."

I jumped back, colliding with Lance. He grasped me before I fell.

"I'm sorry." I apologized.

"I'm not," Lance whispered.

My face reddened, and I turned away. He began unpacking the supplies, and I offered to help.

He handed me a canvas sack and pointed towards the shelter. "Put this inside, it's full of food."

The rest of the supplies he placed next to the lean-to.

"You forgot to pack your book, so I brought it along," he added.

"What book?"

"*Peter Pan*, your name is on the inside page."

I nodded; it was not necessary he know it was a gift from Taylor.

"I did not bring the carved necklace, I recognized Taylor's woodworking skills, I assumed you left it behind on purpose."

I felt tautness in my chest and throat and did not reply.

"I boiled water," I advised. "The container is full, and there's a ruffed grouse in the lean-to. Are we going to eat before we leave?"

Lance shook his head. "It's almost dark, we wouldn't get far. We'll eat, then spend the night here and leave at sunrise. You okay with that?"

I agreed with his suggestion to leave in the morning. The distance I rode since leaving Blackfoot had exhausted me; I decided not to share that information with Lance.

Lance led Ringo and Ginger to where Thunder grazed. He tied Ringo's reins around a tree branch, then he joined me at the fire.

I found a sturdy stick and skewered the grouse. Gripping it above the flames, I turned it periodically to prevent it from searing.

"Smells delicious," Lance announced as he sat cross-legged on the ground. "Besides your tent, I brought a tarp, two flashlights and batteries, and a propane lantern which will come in handy at the cabin. My mother packed cookies, pemmican, and Bannock to eat on the trail. There are plenty of herbs, plants, and Saskatoon berries we can pick on the way."

I lifted my head and watched Lance. He raised his eyebrows.

"Sorry, I didn't mean to stare, it's just that it sounded strange to listen to a person my age discussing their parents, most of the people I've known in the last three years lost them in the earthquake or tsunami."

"Then you, Taylor, Willie, Eddie and Rusty, Debbie and Mai-Li all lost your parents, and managed to escape from Vancouver," he stated.

I nodded in agreement.

"I know Mai-Li lost her parents and brothers, and Taylor told me his father died in the earthquake."

"Yes, he was working and never returned home. Willie's father drowned in the tsunami when his fishing boat sank. He told us his mother left them when he was around ten years old, Eddie and Rusty lost both their parents, and we are not sure about Debbie although the way she clings to Mai-Li, we assumed it was her mother or a female figure."

"And you?"

"My father and mother, and my dog Poppy. I was playing with Poppy in the backyard when the earthquake happened, it frightened her, and she bolted into the trees. I ran after her except I couldn't find her, so I returned to the house, knowing she would have gone back home. There were a gas leak and an explosion, and my parents and Poppy were inside."

Lance stood and placed his hand on my shoulder.

"Carlie, I am so sorry."

"It's finished; I don't usually talk about it. This January was three years since the earthquake. We persevered at Little Mountain for almost two years, and if Taylor hadn't joined our group, none of us would have survived. The cabin was a much-needed reprieve, and losing Rusty was devastating for all of us."

"I don't imagine Willie's behaviour towards you made it any easier."

I shrugged, "When Taylor and Mai-Li insisted I pardon him, I was bitter, but they refused to listen. Taylor took the coward's way out and disappeared without informing me he was leaving with Pete. Mai-Li tried to use her influence to persuade me to concede."

"Thanks for sharing with me, and I can appreciate your anger, and why you don't like to talk about it."

I nodded and stared into the flames.

Lance cleared his throat, then reached for my arm. "You should probably turn that grouse, unless you enjoy eating charcoal."

I gasped and quickly rotated the stick. It was a little charred, but edible.

"I've eaten worse," I mumbled.

"Were you by chance doing the cooking?"

I glared at him, then punched his arm.

"Ow," he muttered. "That hurt."

"Then behave yourself," I warned.

We ate half the grouse and finished the plums. "There's enough left to eat for breakfast tomorrow morning."

Lance nodded, then yawned. "It's late, we should get some sleep, I'd like to leave at daybreak."

I wrapped the leftover meat in the cloth bag I brought with me.

Lance took it, tied a rope around its neck, and flung it around an overhanging branch in a nearby white oak.

"I'll sleep outside tonight," he stated. "There's not enough room in the lean-to for both of us. Tomorrow we will start using the tent."

It was then I realized no sleeping arrangements were made. I entered the lean-to and found my backpack. Tomorrow would begin a new chapter in my life. Had I made the right decision?

Chapter Four

We rose early the next morning and ate the rest of the grouse. Lance retrieved the horses; I helped him repack the pannier and he showed me how to distribute its weight evenly on Ringo's back.

"Now pay attention to what I'm doing, I'm going to saddle Ginger," he instructed me. "Always stand on the left side of the horse, throw the blanket over its back and smooth out any wrinkles and folds, then put on the saddle, and rock it back and forth to make sure it's secure. Unfold the cinch and stirrup, make sure the cinch is secure then pull it down under the belly and slip the strap down through the buckle."

I nodded and took a deep breath, if Lance decided to quiz me, I would be in deep trouble. "Now it's your turn to saddle Thunder."

I approached Thunder's equipment, picked up his saddle; and discovered it was heavier than I expected. I cautiously approached the patient horse, then hesitated as I sensed Lance standing behind me.

"You forget something?" he enquired.

I turned and faced him; a blanket was draped over his arm.

I sighed, put the saddle on the ground, took the wrap, and flung it over Thunder's back. Then I searched for wrinkles and folds, although honestly, I had no idea what I was looking for. I retrieved the saddle and with a groan tossed it over his back. My quick movement surprised him, and he turned sharply. I jumped back, and Lance reached around my shoulder and grabbed the horn.

"I guess I startled him," I admitted.

Lance shook his head. "I should have warned you that might happen; Thunder prefers bareback. He was just assessing you, sometimes he's too smart for his own good. Don't let him win, show him who's in charge."

"I imagine we both know the answer to that," I muttered.

"It'll be a while before you're comfortable around horses," Lance smiled. "Tomorrow, I'll show you how to install the bit and the reins."

Soon we were prepared to leave. "What about the lean-to, shouldn't we take it down?"

"No, the next travellers passing this way might be seeking shelter."

We left the clearing and headed towards a path that followed the river. Lance rode in the lead on Ginger, gripping Ringo's reins in his left hand. I shadowed Ginger on Thunder. When the horses picked up speed, I seized the horn with my left hand and wrapped my right hand tightly around the reins. Lance glanced back and smiled. After what seemed an eternity, he steered away from the trail and into the trees. We rode for a while, then he gestured for me to dismount.

"We'll take a break and refill our canteens," he exclaimed, as he tied Ringo's reins around a tree. "If you require a break, don't wander too far, stay within shouting distance."

I nodded and scurried into the trees. A branch snapped in the heavy bushes, and I quickly finished and headed back to the horses.

I questioned Lance as to where we were going. I told him Taylor always made a point of staying on the paths bordering the streams and the mountains and not take shortcuts through the trees.

"That's probably because he did not know the topography," he replied. "It would have been risky as none of the trails are marked on the maps."

"Shouldn't we worry about wildfires," I probed. Memories of the firestorm we experienced at the Wastelands raced vividly through my mind.

"I'm continuously on alert, watching for hints of smoke or sulphur or observing if the temperature drops suddenly or the wind shifts. If that happens, I'll make a note of the location, then take a different route. You ready to go?"

I nodded, reached for the horn, and struggled to climb up. Lance gestured me to wait. He wandered into the bush and quickly returned, carrying a tree stump, which he set on the ground next to Thunder.

"I meant to do something about this earlier, Thunder's a big horse, and you're, well, a bit close to the ground."

"Are you saying I'm short?"

"Well, if the shoe fits......"

"I am not short," I huffed, "I'm petite."

Lance raised his hands in mock surprise and stepped back. Then he pointed at Thunder's back.

I stood on the stump and cautiously climbed into the saddle. I at once noticed how much easier it was to manoeuvre; I had no intention of admitting that to Lance.

I was drained, and my muscles ached; I was not looking forward to hours of riding. I should have known nothing got by Lance.

"It's normal when apprentice riders feel stiffness and pain in the beginning. You might try straightening your back and relaxing a little, remember not to lean too far forward or backwards, you could lose your balance. Use one hand to control both reins, should you want Thunder to speed up or move ahead, apply light pressure with your heels."

"Won't that hurt him?"

"No worry-wort, it won't."

He untied Thunder's reins, then leaped gracefully on Ginger's back.

"There's so much to learn," I whispered, "I'll never memorize it all."

"It takes practice, as does anything new."

"I suppose being called a worry-wort is better than being called a fussbudget," I muttered under my breath.

Lance snickered, then steered Ginger and Ringo down an overgrown trail. Thunder snorted then picked up his pace. I pulled back on the reins, and he shook his head, straining to keep up with the other horses.

I realized it would take me a while to become accustomed to riding; however, it was a better alternative than hiking all the way.

We stopped around noon, drank a cup of water, and we each ate a delicious blueberry-stuffed Bannock provided by Lance's mother. We guided the horses down to the stream and waited while they drank.

Soon we were back on the trail, we rode most of the afternoon. Dusk was not far off, and Lance gestured towards a grassy field. I sluggishly dismounted, gripped the horn to keep my balance, and leaned on Thunder's shoulder. I watched Lance as he unsaddled Ginger. I fumbled with the cinch and buckle.

Thunder shook his head restlessly and turned in a circle.

"Thunder," Lance warned. The horse at once settled down.

The frustration on my face, and my heavy sighs, did not work on Lance. He waited until I unsecured the cinch and removed the buckle, then he assisted me in removing the saddle, halter, bridle, and reins.

"Do you recall what I told you yesterday, what you have to do next."

"Collapse in a heap on the ground," I answered.

"Before that," he chuckled.

"Um, examine the hoofs and look for stones."

He nodded, then lifted each of Ginger's legs. "She's sound, now, do the same for Thunder."

I approached the enormous horse, clenched his hoof in both my hands, and lifted it. At least, I tried to lift it, except nothing happened. "He won't let me," I snapped.

Lance turned and approached me. "Try again, only be more assertive."

"Assertive," I groaned through clenched teeth.

"Once Thunder is more comfortable with you, he'll start behaving. He's trying to see how far he can push you, don't let him win."

"He's the size of a tank; he'll never listen to me."

"If you don't try, then he's won."

Lance began removing the supplies from Ringo's back. I sighed and tried again to lift

Thunder's hoof; he huffed and remained calm, and I finally succeeded and managed to examine the rest of his hoofs.

"Good boy," I whispered, as I stroked his withers and neck. I raised my head and stared at Lance. "Everything looks okay."

"Excellent, you just passed the first test," he remarked.

Lance tied Ringo to a tree and left Thunder and Ginger untethered.

"Don't you have to rope them too?" I asked.

"They're well trained and won't wander off and will warn us should they pick up the scent of a bear or a cougar in the area."

"Wonderful, lions and tigers and bears, oh my," I mumbled.

Lance gave me the strangest look. "Let's set up the tent first, then we'll start a campfire and eat."

Obviously, *The Wizard of Oz* was not a part of Lance's childhood upbringing.

Being familiar with the small tent, it did not take us long to set up. I silently agreed it was much better than building a lean-to.

I gathered rocks and twigs, and a fire was soon smouldering. Lance handed me a second Bannock, which I devoured, then we finished our meal with strips of pemmican. To my surprise, he removed from his supplies a coffee pot and a tin can carrying coffee grounds.

"Is that real coffee? "I asked.

He opened the canister and sniffed. "Looks like coffee, smells like coffee, it IS coffee."

I laughed aloud and remembered how Mai-Li made us drink chicory when our supply of coffee ran out while hiking to the Interior. I hated it, but when she listed all its benefits, and how healthy it was, I had no choice; it was chicory or boiled water.

After we ate, we used the tack as back props and watched as a comet streaked across the sky. The coffee was brewed, and Lance poured two cups and handed one to me. I inhaled the aroma, took a big gulp, and burnt my tongue.

"Tomorrow we'll hunt small game," he declared. "Maybe rabbit or squirrel."

I swallowed and stared into the flames. "Squirrel?"

"Hmm, superb eating," Lance snickered, obviously enjoying my reaction. "The Bannock and pemmican won't last much longer, and we require something more substantial."

We sat peacefully, absorbing the stillness.

"Time to call it a night," Lance announced. He handed me one of the flashlights and pointed towards the bush. Understanding his message, I nodded, and he headed one way while I went the other. I arrived back at the tent before he did, quickly removed my pyjamas from my backpack and put them on. The air was damp and chilly, and I hastily climbed inside my bag. It wasn't long when I heard Lance moving around outside, then he threw the last dregs of the coffee on the flames and extinguished the fire.

He entered the tent and began to undress. Nervously, I turned and looked away. I heard him crawl inside his sleeping bag.

"Night, Carlie."

"Night."

Exhausted and worn-out, I fell into a deep slumber.

Chapter Five

Lance woke me the next morning; he wanted to leave as soon as possible to make up time we lost when he returned to Blackfoot for supplies. We dismantled the tent and ate the last of the Bannock. I craved a cup of coffee however I understood his hurry.

We finished saddling the horses just as the sun broke through the clouds. We rode in single file and time passed pleasantly. Lance turned and pointed towards a narrow path. "This trail follows one of the smaller creeks, we can't chance crossing the bigger streams because of spring melt-off, the water is high and fast flowing, it would be too dangerous."

"Prior to our group arriving at Blackfoot, we hiked on the Kettle Valley Railway Trail and passed Princeton. It was a flat hike; wouldn't it be easier if we travelled that way?"

"That's because, not only were you walking, but you also had the kids with you, and although it's a longer route, it would have been easier and safer. We'll make better time heading west through the forest. I know where the trails are located."

"Where are we headed?"

"We're travelling northwest, I'm hoping to make it to Blakeburn later in the day, and we'll stay there overnight."

"That's where your grandfather's house is? We stopped there on our way here."

"He told us about your arrival and spending the night there."

"And there's a corral and hay for the horses."

"Wow, what a windfall."

"I guess you knew that already?" I muttered.

Lance laughed softly and urged Ginger forward. Thunder picked up his pace, and I grappled for the horn, rehashing Lance's instructions.

Eventually the creek ended, and the path widened, and we made better time. My back and legs ached, my stomach growled, and I longed for a cup of coffee.

Lance steered the horses off the path, and we climbed a small hill and stopped. Below was a meadow, covered in green grass, dandelions, and wildflowers. I spotted a brook on the far side.

Lance clucked softly and Ginger sprinted downhill; Ringo took the rear. I should have paid closer attention; Thunder had no intention of being left behind. He charged down the hill, and by the time I realized what had happened, I soared over his head and landed heavily on my back. I struggled to catch my breath, then opened my eyes.

Lance was kneeling on the ground beside me. "Carlie, are you hurt?"

"I'm sorry, I wasn't paying attention. I didn't know Thunder was going to take off without any warning."

"It's not your fault, it's mine. I know Thunder well enough to realize he would try to keep up with Ginger and Ringo."

"It's okay."

"No, it's not Carlie, I made a stupid rookie mistake. Can you stand?"

I nodded and tried to sit up. I gasped when I felt a sharp pain on my left side.

"Lance, it's hard to breathe."

"Lie back, keep still, and don't try to move. I'm going to get Ringo; he's carrying the supplies."

Lance leapt on Ginger's back and galloped across the field. He soon returned holding Ringo's reins and removed the supplies from his back. Then he rummaged around until he found a leather pouch.

"Roll on your right side. I know it's painful, I need to look at how badly you're injured."

I did as he requested, and he helped me remove my jacket.

"Can you lift your shirt; I'm going to examine your ribs and back."

The moment he touched me; I jerked sharply and clutched his arm.

Lance nodded then stood. "I don't feel any bumps, it's just a bruised rib or a pulled back muscle, it's not a fracture. Take deep breaths, I'm going down to the stream, the chilly water will keep the swelling down."

"How long are you going to be gone?"

"A few minutes, except you'll need to release me first."

My face turned red, and I lowered my arm.

Lance stood and removed the water container from the supplies. He vaulted on Ginger's back and soon returned. He found a rag and moistened it, then lightly pressed it against my ribs. I inhaled and bit my lower lip.

"I have some pain killers in the medical kit."

When he found them, he handed me two pills and a cup of water and gestured me to swallow.

"What are they?" I asked nervously.

"Acetaminophen, it's safe to take them, you'll heal quicker if I don't wrap your ribs and back."

"How come you know so much about my injury and what to do?"

"With my people, anyone old enough to ride a horse knows basic medical training and First Aid."

"On our journey from Vancouver, we relied on Mai-Li, she knows more about herbs and florae and their healing benefits than anyone I know."

Lance nodded. "You won't be doing any more riding today. I'll set up the tent and make something to eat."

I looked pleadingly at him, and he exhaled noisily. "And I'll brew a pot of coffee."

After the tent was installed, Lance made a campfire. I had no appetite; however, he insisted I eat. He placed the riding equipment behind me and told me to lean back and sit upright as it should lessen the pain. He suggested I remain in that position for the night.

The shadows lengthened, and the light softly faded. I stared into the trees when I heard hooting close. "Great horned owl," Lance revealed.

"Look, there's Mercury and that's Venus. Growing up, Mom, Dad, and I went camping a lot, my dad was interested in the universe and the planets."

I stopped talking and stared into the flames. How I missed them.

"It's going to rain tonight," Lance mentioned, clearing his throat. "We need to take what we can inside the tent and protect the rest of the supplies and tack with the tarp."

Lance supported me when I stood and entered the tent. The pannier, and our backpacks took more than half the space, and the bedrolls the other half. He brought one of the saddles inside and I sat and leaned against it.

"This will support your back," he said. Then he wrapped my camp bag around my arms and legs. "I'll check later to see if you're asleep. If not, then you can try a different position. Sadly, back injuries take time to heal."

"Thanks, Lance. I feel a little better."

"When it rains this time of year, the temperature at night can be cold. Try to sleep if you can, and if you're still in pain tomorrow morning, rather than push it, we'll stay here another day."

I nodded and leaned back.

"We're out of food. I'm going hunting right now," Lance added. "There should be plenty of ducks and rabbits around."

I lifted my head and stared at him.

"I won't go far, you have your rifle, and Thunder will be with you."

I scowled as I glared at Lance.

"He's the best guard horse I have."

"Guard horse," I squeaked.

"He can smell a bear a mile away, and he's big and mean enough to scare them off."

I exhaled loudly, conjuring up the prospect of meeting a bear. "As long as it's not a cougar or a cheetah," I muttered.

Lance scowled, obviously wondering if I was delirious and why I harboured such a fascination for wildcats.

Chapter Six

I woke the next morning to a mouthwatering aroma of meat and freshly brewed coffee. When Lance left last night to hunt, I had immediately fallen asleep and did not hear him return.

I leaned forward and moaned. I was stiff and ached everywhere. The tent flap opened, and Lance lowered his head and stepped inside. He looked at me and frowned. "You don't look too perky, I suppose there's no sense questioning how you feel. Breakfast is almost done, you hungry?"

I nodded and leaned back. "I'm not that hungry, but I'm really thirsty."

"You can have coffee AFTER you eat some food, then we will pack the horses and ride to Blakeburn. I know you're still in pain, thankfully we don't have a long ride ahead of us. It's going to rain again tonight, and the cabin will be warmer than the tent."

Lance stepped outside and at once returned, carrying a plate of meat smothered in gravy. "It's quail, eat as much as you can, it's essential you keep your energy high."

I ate slowly and when I finished, he took my plate and handed me a mug of coffee.

"While I take down the tent and start packing, move around and stretch as much as you can, it will loosen your muscles."

I strolled unhurriedly around the campsite; my hands wrapped tightly around the hot mug. The tension in my back eased, and I felt slightly better. Lance packed the tent and supplies, and it was not long when we were prepared to leave.

I stood on the tree stump; he helped me mount Thunder. "If you are in a lot of discomfort, let me know, and I'll wrap your ribs and back."

The horses jogged across the meadow, and we arrived at a narrow trail. We travelled at a slow pace, and I gripped the reins tightly.

Lance formed a single line, Ginger in front and Ringo keeping pace with the well-trained horse. When Thunder tried to join them, he picked up his pace, and Lance turned and raised his voice, commanding him to reduce his speed.

The sun peeked around a cloud, and the massive trees cast shadows on the ground. Fragrant plants sprouted blossoms; we passed a thicket of Saskatoon berries. It would not be long when they were ripe and ready to be picked.

At times Lance left the trail, and we wove our way through the dense forest and thick foliage. Tree branches creaked and leaves rustled when a light breeze coiled around the gigantic trunks. A disturbed whiskey jack announced his displeasure, squirrels chattered noisily when we intruded too close to their nests, and I heard the rustle of an animal foraging in the underbrush.

We arrived at a new trail, and Lance stopped and pointed ahead. "That stream is a runoff from Blakeburn Creek, we're almost at my grandfather's cabin."

My thoughts returned to when we stopped in the deserted town. I recalled the creek located behind Pete's house. He invited us to dinner and suggested we spend the night and continue our journey in the morning. We pitched our tents next to the brook; the sky had been shrouded with dark clouds and the surrounding landscape buried beneath blowing snow.

We turned a corner, and I spotted the desolate dwellings and barns. The surroundings were disparate from our previous visit with Pete; I glanced at the ground, buried in grass and wildflowers; the budding branches on the trees rustled in a gentle breeze.

I tailed Lance down the weathered road to Pete's house. The horses did not require encouragement to enter the corral. Lance helped me dismount, restraining Thunder's reins to keep him from joining his companions. I used the saddle horn as a leverage and recoiled when an agonizing spasm radiated down my back.

"How bad is it?" Lance asked.

"My whole-body aches," I answered.

"You will feel better once you take a couple of pain killers. I'll start the wood stove and heat some water; a hot bath will loosen your muscles."

"I'm sorry you're stuck doing everything," I apologized.

"When I'm thrown off Ginger, then you can take care of me."

"As if that'll happen," I mumbled.

"What, you wouldn't take care of me if I got hurt?"

"Of course, I would, it's just that I don't imagine there's any chance of you being thrown off Ginger."

Lance chuckled. "You'd be surprised, most people, no matter how well they ride, can fall or get thrown off a horse."

He pointed towards the cabin. "I'll help you inside, then I'll unpack and feed the horses."

He assisted me when I climbed the steps leading to the porch, then he opened the door, and I strode behind him into the family room. I sat down on the leather couch.

"How come the door wasn't locked?" I questioned.

"People out here seldom lock their doors. Even when they're not home, anyone passing through is welcome to take shelter. I imagine it's different living in huge towns or cities; most people would be anxious and exposed if their doors were unlocked. Padlocking them provides false security from unknown threats," Lance answered.

"That's what it was like growing up in Vancouver," I said. "We didn't know our neighbours, everyone was so occupied. I suppose surviving on my own after the earthquake made me distrustful of strangers."

"An interesting topic, but we'll talk about it later if you want," Lance suggested. He wandered into the kitchen, took a glass from the cupboard, and filled it with water from his flask. "Drink this, it'll relax your muscles, I'll return after I take care of the horses."

I leaned back on the couch, sipping the water. I closed my eyes and sat up in alarm when the back door opened. Lance entered carrying the satchel with our supplies and food. "I've stored the equipment in the back porch, along with our weapons."

He went into the kitchen and set the rucksack on the floor. There was a direct view into the room from where I sat. I recalled the time we stopped here on our way to Blackfoot and had a meal with Pete. He shared his premonitions with us and after speaking to me, left me perplexed and angry *"...you find it difficult to share your affection with someone who loves you, you must overcome your doubts and fears if you choose to be happy. That choice, of course, is yours."* I had not thought about his omen since that time, was Pete's insight true?

Lance retrieved a tall container sitting on the floor next to the sink. "There's a water pump in the back yard," he explained as he left the kitchen and headed towards the back door.

"Can I help with anything?" I offered.

"You are in no shape to do anything right now. I'll make something to eat shortly; we can finish off the quail."

"Are we out of food?"

Lance shook his head. "No, Grandfather keeps his root cellar stocked all year round, it's built into the side of a hill in the back yard and is made from heavy rocks, stones, and wood. The door is heavy enough to keep the animals out. There should be plenty of vegetables, fruit, jerky, and smoked meat, we won't go hungry."

I told Lance about the time I survived on my own in a root cellar at Little Mountain, and how it kept me warm and safe during the winter.

He stared at me the longest time before he left the cabin. He soon returned with the metal bucket and returned to the kitchen. When he opened the damper on the wood stove, I heard rustling and clanging, then the clunk of kindling and logs being placed inside the ashpan.

"If you're able, you might as well join me, we can eat while the stove is heating," Lance called. I limped into the kitchen and sat at the table. He struck a match and tossed it inside the stove. We ate in comfortable silence. Halfway through our meal, Lance poured water into a large metal container and placed it on the burner.

"There's an outhouse in the back not far from the cabin," Lance informed, interrupting my thoughts. "The bedrooms have chamber pots that can be used at night."

By the time we finished eating, the water was boiling. Lance helped me walk back to the couch, then returned to the kitchen and removed the container from the stove. He wandered to the back of the family room and opened the door on the left and went inside. He soon returned carrying the empty metal container.

"There's a metal bathtub in Grandfather's bedroom," he informed me, noticing my puzzled look. "I'll heat more water, then you can take a bath. It should help relieve your constricted back muscles. I'll use the same bathwater after you're finished."

Lance filled the tub halfway with hot water, then added two small buckets of cooler water. "Bath's ready," he announced.

He picked up my backpack, and I followed him to Pete's bedroom. Lance handed me a towel, turned, and left.

There was a double bed against the back wall, and a night table with a propane lantern sitting on top. A three-drawer dresser was found next to the bed. I recognized Pete's workmanship.

The tub was in the far corner under a picture window. There was a small table with a wash basin, a jug of water, and a tin cup. I rummaged through my pack until I found my soap and shampoo, relieved I had packed them before I left Blackfoot.

I undressed, then awkwardly climbed in. The hot water was soothing and relaxing; I sighed and closed my eyes. It would not be long, and I would be living by myself without the luxury and comfort of power, running water or bathrooms. Not having the amenities at my disposal did not overly stress me; however, the idea of living on my own left me anxious and tense. I survived almost two years on my own on Little Mountain; would I have the stamina and strength to do it again at the cabin?

Taylor's face flashed before my eyes; I stiffened and angrily shook my head. I fought against the underlying emotions I felt. My anger was intense, and once again I was reminded of Pete's omen.

Chapter Seven

After Lance bathed, he emptied and cleaned the tub. He took me to a second bedroom and helped me carry my supplies and backpack inside.

Then he hurried to the root cellar and returned with potatoes, canned fruit, and a smoked ham. He placed them on the kitchen table and joined me in the living room. I was lying on the couch; a warm quilt wrapped around my shoulders.

"We'll check tomorrow morning to see if you're well enough to travel," he explained.

"You don't expect I'll be able to ride?"

"The longest part of our journey is ahead of us, we'll leave when you're ready, okay?"

I nodded unhappily, realizing I was the reason for our delay. Noticing my reaction, Lance came and sat beside me on the couch.

"You need to stop blaming yourself, it was an accident, it could have happened to anyone."

"Won't your family be worried about you if you're gone too long?"

"This is not the first time I have been on my own, I have been on spirit quests, and I often accompanied Grandfather on his expeditions. He taught me about nature, gathering food and medicines. The Learning Circle, produced years ago by the First Nations people in Canada instructed our children about Indigenous ways. We developed a deeper appreciation and comprehension of the land and the modifications that are a result of climate change. If I were injured, I would find a way to send a message."

"Your education is different from what I experienced growing up," I mentioned.

Lance stood and strolled to the bookshelf. "We attended regular school from an early age," he added, turning to look at me. "We learned the basics: reading, writing and arithmetic; to live in the New World, we must also learn how to survive with nature."

"Why do you call it the New World?" I questioned.

"I wondered how long it would take you to ask me that."

He skimmed through the book titles and found what he was searching for. "Aha, here it is. I started reading this book six months ago, one of these days I'll finish it." Then he went and sat in a comfortable armchair next to the fireplace.

"The New World," Lance replied. "Hmmm, let me see. Because of the decline of Earth's natural resources, man must change. Environmental recovery is imperative, we need healthier ecosystems, lifestyle changes, and self-sufficiency in connecting with nature. One of the major concerns is depletion of resources caused by climate change, but that's just the beginning."

"I imagine through work and effort, people can learn flexibility," I affirmed. "It's something we do, not something we have."

"That's true and being open to new ideas and letting go of the old ways is one way of stepping out of your comfort zone."

I could have spent the night talking about this topic with Lance; I felt my eyelids droop and realized it was time to call it a night.

"I'm going to bed," I announced as I stood and headed towards the spare bedroom.

"Take two of the pills, it should relieve some of the pain so you can rest better. I left the bottle on the night table. We can discuss this matter later when you're feeling better."

I nodded, then closed the door. I opened my backpack, poured water into the basin, and brushed my teeth. I missed the taste of toothpaste and accepted a long time ago it was an unattainable luxury from my past. I took the two Acetaminophen as instructed and crawled under the blankets.

I rehashed my conversation with Lance, was he cautioning me how to survive on my own, to let go of my old ways and to be prepared to step out of my comfort zone? I recalled the discussions Taylor, Mai-Li and I shared during the long winter nights in the cabin. Taylor believed adaptation was a skill humans must acquire to deal with constant alterations in the world.

I tossed and turned and eventually fell into a troubled sleep. My muscles were stiff and sore when I woke in the morning. I threw back the covers and hobbled to the window.

The leaves and grass sparkled with raindrops, and I smiled when a white-tailed doe and her newborn wandered into the yard. The fawn was ruddy brown with mottled white spots; the doe groomed her baby as it suckled, periodically lifting her head, alert to any disturbance or danger.

I dressed in my blue jeans and sweater and made a mental note to do laundry when I arrived at the cabin. It was a chore I detested, in comparison, I would only have myself to worry about and not six other people. I stopped abruptly and took a deep breath, fighting the wrenching gut feeling and tightness in my chest. Taylor, Mai-Li, and the children were no longer a part of my life.

I heard a bang and a muttered curse; I left the bedroom and headed towards the sounds emanating from the kitchen. Lance was standing next to the counter, clutching a spatula in his hand. The woodstove was lit, and a cast iron fry pan was sitting on the front burner. The kitchen smelled of grease and something charred. At that moment, I did not have the courage to question what he was cooking, and wisely said nothing.

"Can I help?" I asked, restraining my laughter.

Lance raised his head and sputtered angrily. "Do I look as if I need it?"

I shook my head, then reached for the spatula. "I'll finish frying the potatoes and whatever this is, and you can make the coffee."

"Fine, I'll open the windows, it's hard to breathe in here."

Once again, I wisely held my tongue.

"And it's ham, okay?" Lance sputtered. "Where's the coffee pot?"

I pointed to the counter and stirred the mixture in the frying pan. It wasn't long before we sat at the table, eating partially cooked potatoes, burnt ham and drinking strong coffee.

"How are you feeling this morning?" Lance enquired.

"A bit stiff and sore, although I'm better than yesterday."

He nodded and scraped his plate with his fork. "We'll stay one more day and leave tomorrow."

He finished his coffee and poured a second cup. I lifted my mug in the air; he smiled and refilled it. It was quiet in the kitchen while we drank.

"I'm going to water and feed the horses," Lance informed me as he pushed back his chair. "Then I'll come back and tidy up this mess."

"Lance, I'm well enough to clean the kitchen, then I'll take it easy the rest of the day. Take your time with the horses."

Not needing further persuasion, he shrugged and left. I washed the dishes, scrubbed the frying pan, the stove top, the counter, the sink, and the kitchen table. How could one man make such a mess in half an hour?

The rest of the day passed peacefully, Lance read his book, and I took a long nap and felt better when I woke. When he returned his book to the shelf, he noticed a piece of paper stuffed between two books. "I found my map," he exclaimed. "I misplaced it ages ago, I wondered where it ended up?"

"Obviously you didn't need it," I commented. "You seem to know your way around."

"I do, I'll leave it with you at the cabin, and one day it might come in handy."

That night we packed our bags, and Lance went to the root cellar and returned with canned fruit, potatoes, raw carrots, apples, pemmican, dried beans, and chestnuts.

"I'm bringing enough food to tide us over until we arrive at the cabin, we can hunt along the way and pick wild herbs and berries."

We woke early the next morning, ate a quick breakfast, and left. A damp mist clung to our hair and clothing, and I inhaled the earthy scents of pine and greenery, which created an atmosphere of unnatural silence. Weather in May could be unpredictable in the mountains, and I hoped the sun would make an appearance.

I turned and studied the deserted town. At one point, it must have been a productive bustling village, and I visualized people on horseback, strolling down the streets, children running and playing in the yards. I recalled stopping at the ghost town of Granite City on our hike to the Interior. Taylor often expressed his interest in the deserted mining and gold towns and hoped one day to explore and write about them. He felt people living in overpopulated, noisy, fast-paced cities would return to the smaller communities or homesteads. Blackfoot was a prime example of a healthier option by reconnecting with the land and nature.

We rode through the dense forest, surrounded by thick ferns and swaying wildflowers. The raw earthy scent of the wet earth permeated my senses. We passed massive pine trees and cedars; the budding leaves were a vigorous shade of green. The horses side-stepped the gnarled roots on the path; acorns and pine needles crunched under their hooves. Rays of mellow sunlight penetrated the leaves, and the occasional chirp of a bird or the chatter of a noisy squirrel interrupted the silence. I spotted the intense blue feathers of a stellar jay as it landed on a branch and noisily announced its presence.

We rode at a leisurely pace, and eventually Blakeburn Creek ended. The path narrowed, and Lance steered Ginger and Ringo towards an open field obscured by dandelions. Bearing in mind Thunder's impulsiveness to keep pace with his companions, I tightened my grasp on the reins.

We headed towards a fallen tree trunk. Lance assisted me when I dismounted, I swayed, he held my waist, then lowered me to the ground.

"Carlie, are you okay?"

"Just a bit dizzy," I answered. "I'm not used to riding long distances, that's all."

"Or you're not as well as you implied you were."

I closed my eyes and shrugged, choosing to ignore his remark.

"I'm going to tether the horses in the trees; they fancy dandelions and unfortunately Thunder doesn't know when to stop eating them. The last thing we need is a colicky horse."

He soon returned, carrying the backpack. "I'll start a fire, and we'll have something to eat. Rest a while, and then we'll find out how you feel."

It wasn't long before a pot of coffee brewed, and I inhaled the aroma. Lance opened a can of peaches and handed me a spoon. I flinched when I took it from him.

"Is something wrong?"

"This just brings back long-buried memories. On our trek to the Interior, we found a cache of canned peaches and Mai-Li handed out spoons to each of us and we ate standing up. The kids thought it was hilarious. I don't know why I remembered that."

"You mourn the loss of your comrades, especially the kids. It will take time to accept their absence."

After we ate, I handed the empty peach can to Lance, and he stuffed it inside a garbage bag. I threw the coffee grounds on the flames.

Soon we were back on the trail. A sunbeam broke through the dense trees, and I heeded the rustling sounds of animals scurrying under the thick ferns.

"Are we close to the Tanglewood Hills?" I asked.

Lance shook his head. "That's out of our way; the cabin is south of here. We should arrive sometime tomorrow."

"That's right, I forgot. We took the northern route because we originally planned to go to Princeton. Then I got injured, and Mai-Li suggested we go to Blackfoot instead, as there were healers there."

We rode at a leisurely pace, hours later, Lance turned down a side path, and I heard the soothing sound of a rippling brook. He led the horses through lush greenery, and we arrived at a clearing. An owl hooted close by, and the sounds of croaking frogs and chirping crickets interrupted the silence.

Lance removed the gear from Ringo's back. I assisted in setting up the tent and searched for branches and twigs to fuel a fire. We ate in silence while he stared solemnly at the flickering flames.

I topped off his mug with coffee, then poured myself a second cup. I was uncomfortable, as it was clear something was bothering him.

Lance finished drinking his coffee. Then he cleared his throat. "Carlie, I have a question, and it's important you be totally honest with me?"

His grave tone put me on alert.

"Are you sure you can make it on your own at the cabin?"

I was unprepared and at a loss how to answer.

"You don't believe I can do it?" I snapped harshly as I lowered myself to the ground.

"That's not what I asked."

I stared directly at him, conflicted and uneasy.

"I have no choice, Lance," I replied bitterly. "I have nowhere else to go, I must make it work."

He was silent, then stood and doused the flames with water.

"Let's call it a night, we'll wake up early and ride straight to the cabin. We have a long day ahead of us."

I detected the anger in his voice, and if he was not prepared to discuss it further, then neither was I. I survived on my own in the past, and I would do it again.

Chapter Eight

We rose early the next morning and ate a quick breakfast. We dismantled the tent and packed the supplies. Lance had not spoken to me since our conversation last night. Exhausted and on-edge, I did not rest well. Once we arrived at the cabin, there would be nothing stopping him from returning, his duties and responsibilities would end.

We rode hours in silence, and the creaking saddles and the clip-clop of horses' hooves were the only sounds announcing our presence in the idyllic setting. We wound our way through the thick trees and arrived at the Hudson Bay Company Trail. We were close to the Tulameen River crossing; by early afternoon, we would arrive at the junction to the cabin.

I was stiff and sore and stubbornly refused to ask Lance to stop. I recognized our location when we arrived at the turnoff. Heading north, we reached the furrowed road, and after riding a short distance, it disappeared, and we were back on the narrow path.

We turned a corner and faced the cabin. I stared in dismay at the depleted wood pile, the yard littered with garbage, broken bottles, and empty beer cans. I recalled when we originally found the cabin, and the disgusting condition it was in. We worked weeks making it liveable.

Lance rode to the steps and dismounted. He motioned me to stay, and he cautiously entered the cabin. It was not long when he joined me.

"It's been occupied, and definitely requires cleaning," he grumbled, breaking the silence. "The woodstove has been knocked over and disassembled; hopefully I'll find all the missing parts and it's still intact."

I nodded, dismounted, and flinched, belatedly ignoring my injury. Lance noticed my reaction and did not comment. I climbed the steps, opened the door, and stepped inside. Plastic wrappers, food scraps, soot, and dirt littered the floor. I wandered to the shed and opened the door, hoping the supplies were not stolen or destroyed. I was not surprised to find the wood pile gone. I sighed in relief when I noticed the folded bear skin lying on the top shelf. It was then I realized I did not have an axe, why did not I bring one with me. I was distressed and furious when I left, the only provisions I packed were what I had in the house.

I left the shed and returned to the main room. Lance was leaning against the kitchen counter. He crossed his arms and watched as I went to the table and sat down on one of the wood seats. Thankfully, they were still intact and had not been burned as firewood.

"Are you okay?" he questioned.

I stared at the table; my stomach tied in knots.

"No Lance, I am not okay. This place is a pigsty, the wood is gone, most of the supplies are missing or stolen, and I do not have an axe or any matches. I won't be able to start a fire, although I don't know why I am worried about that anyway as I don't have an axe."

Lance chuckled softly and sat down next to me. He reached over and took my hands. "You need to settle down, and it's not that tricky to start a fire, with or without matches."

"I tried before, I rubbed two sticks together and it didn't work."

Lance turned his head and looked out the back window. I could have sworn his shoulders were shaking, was he laughing at me?

"Carlie, have you ever used a flint kit."

"Taylor owned one, and he showed me how to use it."

"Problem solved, I have one as well and will show you again how it works. You okay with that?"

"I know you don't believe I can make it on my own," I answered bitterly. "You made that clear last night, and I guess I just proved you right."

"You made a mistake, something we all do. I have no intention of abandoning you," he assured me, turning to face me. "Especially when you require assistance."

"It's my fault," I interrupted. "I was not prepared. I should have bought an axe, and a flint kit before I left. I was so upset when Mai-Li told me I had to leave without Eddie, I wasn't thinking straight."

"I have an axe, we can replace the missing wood, and I'll give you some pointers on how to start a fire, with a flint and without a flint."

"Lance, I really appreciate your kindness, and I imagine you had no intention of prolonging your stay."

"Carlie, your back is not healed, you can't lift anything heavy, you're in no shape to be left on your own. If I deserted you, Grandfather would be extremely disappointed in me and would disown me. When the cabin is liveable, and you're comfortable being on your own, then I'll leave."

I nodded, contemplating the doubtful event Pete would deny the existence of his only grandson.

"Since you haven't answered I'm assuming you're in agreement with my offer?" Lance questioned.

"Yes," I muttered awkwardly.

"Then that's settled. When you're prepared to stay here on your own, and I know it's time to leave, I will ask you again. You must be honest with me, I have no way of knowing if you are, the choice of course will be yours and I will not interfere."

I nodded, thankful and relieved.

"The first thing on our agenda is food; before I leave, I'll remove the supplies and water the horses at the creek, then I'll hobble Ringo and Thunder next to the cabin, there's plenty of grass and I'll feed them before I leave."

I followed him outside and watched as he finished his chores, then he joined me on the porch. He mounted Ginger, leaned forward, catching my attention. "If you're looking for something to do while I'm gone, inspect the outhouse and check the shape it's in. I imagine it will demand a thorough cleaning, try and make it useable for tonight, just don't overdo it."

I scrunched my face, Lance chuckled and steered Ginger into the woods.

I strode to the outhouse and pushed open the door. The stench was overpowering, although I had confronted worse when I survived on Little Mountain. I grabbed the bucket from the shed and strode to the stream. I considered Lance's advice, and half-filled it with water. My back was throbbing by the time I climbed the hill three times and finished the repulsive task of cleaning the outside privy. I entered the cabin and inspected the kitchen cupboards. The dishes and cutlery were still intact, and when my back improved, the first thing I intended to do was boil water and scour everything. Hopefully, it wouldn't take Lance long to fix the stove. I dragged up the memory of the washing and added that to my list.

I found the broom and dustpan leaning against the back wall of the shed. Considering the state of the cabin, the trespassers did obviously not use it. I removed as much of the dirt and mud as I could, nevertheless, it was clear it would take a lot of scrubbing to make the cabin and shed sanitary.

I left by the back door and staggered down the hill to Taylor's wood shop. I smiled when I found one of Debbie's ribbons and a bag of nails Eddie stashed under a pile of wood. I remembered their laughter, and Taylor's patience in keeping them entertained.

I ambled towards the creek; the water was flowing rapidly from the spring snowmelt. Thankfully there seemed no threat of flooding.

I heard my name being called, I climbed the hill and spotted Lance striding towards the shed. He waved and waited while I joined him. He opened his leather bag, and I noticed two grouse.

"Grab one of the birds, we'll leave the other one in the shed, it should be cold enough tonight to keep until tomorrow."

I stayed close by when he entered the cabin. "I notice you've been working," he added.

"I swept the floors although what's really required is a vigorous scrubbing; I cleaned the soot and ground-in dirt and got rid of the broken bottles and beer cans. The privy was in half-decent shape; I ran out of energy, so I'll tackle it again tomorrow."

"How's your back?"

"A bit sore; I've been careful not to overdo."

"I'll hobble the three horses in the front yard for tonight. The first thing I intend to work on is the woodstove. Hopefully, I'll find the missing parts, and once I've repaired it, then I'll give it a thorough cleaning. The nights are still cold; we still need it."

I turned to leave. "Can you start a campfire and cook the grouse?" Lance requested.

I nodded and headed towards the door.

"Whoa, wait a minute," Lance countered. "Take this."

"What is it?"

"My flint kit, we'll go to bed hungry tonight if you plan on rubbing two sticks together."

I grumbled, turned to leave, and caught sight of a dishrag on the table. I grabbed it and threw it at him. He did not duck quick enough, and it landed on his head.

I laughed and reached for the doorknob, Lance not far behind. I dropped the bird in my haste; he grabbed my waist and turned me slowly. He stared into my eyes, then he released me, cleared his throat, and handed me his kit.

Retrieving the grouse, I rushed outside and headed towards the firepit. The stack of firewood was gone, and ashes and burnt tinder and debris were scattered around the yard. I found discarded clothing and a pair of beat-up boots. It distressed me when people showed no remorse in leaving deserted cabins or shelters in such disarray. I gathered tinder, twigs and needles and started a fire, using the rubbish as kindling. I plucked and cleaned the grouse and waited until the flames burned down, then held it over the coals.

Concern raced through my mind as I stared into the trees. What just happened? When Taylor rejected me, I made a promise to myself I would not be involved with anyone until I decided what to do with my life.

Would my decision to withdraw from the world and embrace solitude help me find what I required and desired? I realized the only way I would find happiness was to stop relying on others, and to have confidence in myself. Whether or not I chose the more favourable path, I convinced myself that having close friends was not as important as people believed or declared it to be. If I intended to find peace and contentment, living on my own was a crucial step in the process.

Chapter Nine

The cabin door opened, and Lance strolled over and joined me at the campfire. He had removed his buckskin jacket and was bare chested.

"I'm finished with the stove, we all set to eat?"

I nodded and reached across the coals and removed the grouse.

"I'm covered in soot and dirt," he forewarned, "Give me time to wash up at the creek, I won't be long."

I hurried to the cabin; the grilled meat burnt my fingers, and I placed it on a platter I found in the cupboard.

I set the table and discovered a can of cherries hidden in the back cupboard, which we somehow missed when we left the cabin after Christmas. I found the can opener and opened it, the berries had survived, and I poured them into a plastic bowl.

Lance soon returned to the cabin and sat down at the table.

"Looks yummy, I'm starving," he mentioned.

"I didn't use any of your grandfather's food," I added, avoiding eye contact. "I found a can of cherries; they should be good."

"Works for me."

After we ate, Lance stood and returned to the shed. I cleared the table and stacked the plates in the sink.

He soon returned carrying the firebox of the wood stove, and after a few quick trips, he retrieved the remaining parts, which he spread on the floor.

As there was limited room in the cabin, I went to the sink and washed the dishes in freezing water, then sat at the table and watched as Lance finished reinstalling the stove. He stood and wiped his hands on a rag.

"We won't start it tonight; we'll wait until tomorrow morning. There'll be a lot of smoke when we start it up."

"It's still not that warm at night," I said.

"It's not bad, we have our bedrolls, and if we get cold, we can always fight over the bearskin."

Then he strode over to the large mattress and dug through his backpack and recovered his jacket. He turned and went outside to the porch and sat on the top step.

I followed him and thanked him for fixing the stove. He nodded and gestured for me to sit next to him. His buckskin jacket was draped over his arm, and he held a brush in his right hand. I watched him closely, and he noticed my interest. "Cleaning my clothing is a daily ritual. In this case, I removed as much of the dirt and soot as I could, and once the stove is working, I'll heat water and handwash my jacket and leggings. Then it's only a matter of air drying them in the shade."

"That's a lot of work every time you do laundry," I commented.

"Actually, it's worth it. Buckskin is comfortable to wear, is extremely resilient and lasts a long time," he replied. "It's good in both warm and cool climates and is water resistant."

"I guess you don't worry about carrying a lot of clothing when you travel," I added.

Lance nodded in agreement. "Buckskin is also handy when we hunt and move around dense forests and on steep cliffs, it protects the wearer from thorns, branches, and rocks. Besides clothing, we use buckskin to make pouches, belts, and moccasins. Nothing is wasted."

The sun disappeared behind a cloud, and I rose. "Lance, can you bring the backpacks inside, I might as well start putting things away?"

"I'll bring them in shortly; I'm almost finished brushing my jacket."

I returned inside and checked the beds and willow mattresses and shuddered when I thought of who might have slept there last. Lance could take Taylor's and Eddie's old bed, mine was still against the wall behind the front door.

Lance soon appeared carrying the backpacks and supplies and stacked them on the table.

"Come sit a minute," he mentioned. "I have something I want to show you."

He removed a box from his pack and placed it on the table. "Go ahead, open it."

I unfolded the side flaps and reached inside and emptied the contents and spread them on the table. I gasped and struggled to breathe. "It's paper, and pencils."

Lance nodded. "There's also paint and brushes."

"Oh my God," I whispered. "Is this for me?"

Lance nodded and laughed.

"Thank you, thank you, this is amazing."

"I see you approve. Once you're settled in, you'll have extra time on your hands; you might as well work on your art. I know how much you love drawing and painting."

"And these," he said pointing to a pile of blank pamphlets. "Can be used for sketching flowers, animals, and scenery."

"I love it," I exclaimed, throwing my arms around his neck. I froze and stepped back.

"I'm sorry," I whispered.

"I'm not," Lance replied.

I blushed and looked at the floor. "I can't wait to start."

"It's getting late, let's unpack the supplies then make the beds," Lance suggested. "The less propane we burn the longer it will last."

We spent the next hour unpacking.

"You still doing the wash tomorrow?" Lance asked.

I nodded and threw my dirty clothes in a pile, then Lance added a few items. I recalled our conversation about the advantages of wearing buckskin. It wouldn't be a bad idea if I started wearing it as well. I shook my head, no, there was no way I could ever replace my blue jeans, shirts, or my lined jacket. In any event, by the time I learned how to tan buckskin, I would be an old lady in a rocking chair.

I spread open the sleeping bags on the mattresses, and Lance retrieved the bearskin from the shed. "Use this until the stove is safe to ignite."

"Okay, thanks," I replied.

I headed to the shed to change into my pj's and quickly returned to the main room, raced across the floor, and climbed inside the sleeping bag and pulled up the bearskin.

Lance carried the propane lantern to the mattress and removed his shirt. He started to untie the strap around his leggings, and I turned my head and faced the wall.

The moonlight shone into the dark, rustic room, adding an ambience of peace and tranquillity.

I was weary, and my back and ribs ached. I tossed and turned, trying to find a comfortable position.

"You still hurting?" Lance inquired.

"A little," I whispered. "I should be okay after I get a good night's sleep."

"Night, Carlie."

"Night Lance."

Chapter Ten

The next morning, Lance started the woodstove, and I opened the back window half-way to clear the smoke from the room. I poured water into the kettle and sat it on the burner. As I did not have a lot of clothes to wash, I decided to launder them in the kitchen sink rather than haul everything down to the stream, which is what I did when our group of six resided at the cabin. I had hauled our soiled clothing down to the stream, pounded them against a rock and rinsed them in the icy water. It was not only time-consuming but brutal work as well. My fingers ached from the cold, and it took me hours to warm up. When the wintry weather finally arrived, we melted the snow in a metal bucket, and I washed the clothes in the shed.

I scrounged through the cupboards and drawers and finally located the ropes we used as clotheslines and strung them up in the shed.

Lance spent the morning cutting trees and chopping wood, and I stacked the logs in the shed.

"Let's take a break and have something to eat," he suggested.

I decided to save the rest of the grouse for supper. "You okay if we eat the rest of the pemmican and crackers, and there's canned fruit left?"

Lance nodded, and I set the food on the table. I poured each of us a cup of water, then refilled the kettle and set it on the stove to boil.

"Once the wood has been replaced, and the cabin, shed and the privy are cleaned, we should think about tracking down a deer or moose."

When I did not respond, Lance leaned back and looked directly at me. "You mentioned you hunted with Taylor, so you know what's involved."

I shrugged, I knew if I intended to stay at the cabin on my own, it would be necessary to have a backup supply of food and meat on hand. I could hunt small-game animals and ptarmigan, quail, or pheasants, but larger game was out of my reach.

"If you decide it's more than you can take on, Carlie, there is always the possibility of working and moving in with settlers or homesteaders, as I suggested earlier. Alternatively, going to Princeton is still a proposal, but only as a last resort."

"I know, I have spent time brooding about it and realize the best way to earn independence is to live alone, and if I can't, I'll never be happy being with anyone. I know it won't be simple; however, I must try."

"I have confidence in your abilities, although I suspect you're taking on more than you can manage."

"I must do this if I want Eddie back. Taylor and Mai-Li are no longer in my life. I will not and cannot absolve Willie; no-one knows what I endured."

Lance did not respond.

"Leaving Little Mountain was due to Taylor's perceptiveness," I added. "At times our journey was brutal and heart-breaking, but eventually we arrived in Blackfoot."

"Do you know if any of the people living at Little Mountain survived?" Lance remarked.

I shook my head. "When we decided to leave, many had already headed north. We discussed that alternative as well as we were aware the Interior was closed to vagrants. Mai-Li informed us her family was there, and we would all be welcome."

Lance nodded.

"I have no idea if there are any survivors left, most of the food and uncontaminated water was gone." I continued. "When we reached the Wastelands, we clashed with the Desert Rats. Their leader Lars swore he would settle a score with Taylor because we stole three of their rifles and some ammunition. There originally was bad blood between them when Taylor challenged him for leadership of the Phantoms, the largest and strongest gang who had control of the Bloedel Conservatory at Little Mountain. Lars was forced to leave when Taylor succeeded.

The Desert Rats tracked us inland and caught up with us somewhere between Peers Creek and the Sowaqua Creek Trailhead. When the rest of the Desert Rats were made aware of Rusty's death, they refused to support Lars and told him they were turning around and going back to the Wastelands. Taylor convinced Lars to do the same; the weather had turned cold; snow was expected at any time. Taylor was heavily armed, and Lars was quite aware, he would not come out the winner if he challenged Taylor."

"What finally convinced him to turn around?"

"Taylor told him he did not intend to return to the Wastelands as he had no interest in the Desert Rats. Lars accepted Taylor's decision, and he and his gang turned around and left."

"Do you imagine that's the last you've seen of Lars?"

I shrugged my shoulders. "I remember Mai-Li questioning Taylor if he trusted him, and Taylor admitting he never did and never would."

"Does Lars know where the cabin is?" Lance asked.

"He knows nothing about the cabin; he was obviously tracking us and had assumed we were hiking to the Interior. The

Wastelands is a long way from here, and other than the stolen weapons, we had nothing of theirs that would make it worthwhile for them to trail us. I can't imagine the Desert Rats trying to search for us again, the number of weapons we took were not worth the trouble."

"I'm not worried about the Desert Rats, it's Lars that bothers me," Lance added. "A man carrying a personal grudge often resists letting it go, to him it is an unresolved issue. Why did you not divulge this earlier?"

"It never came to mind; I just thought about him when we spoke about Little Mountain and our journey to the Interior."

"This alters the situation, Carlie. If Lars ever finds you alone, you will not be able to defend yourself."

"It's Taylor he's desperate to locate, not me."

"What better way to make Taylor suffer than to harm the woman he cares for?" Lance asserted through gritted teeth. "I will stay until I know you are able to protect yourself, then and only then will I leave."

I lowered my head, suddenly realizing I was crying. Lance reached over and took me in his arms. I clung to him. He held me rigidly, then I pushed back, and wiped my face with the back of my hand.

"You know I am here for you," Lance murmured. "But you still have a lot to learn if you insist on remaining here on your own."

"I know, and I appreciate your assistance, at times it's so overwhelming, and I wonder if I am doing the right thing."

"Only you know the answer to that, Carlie, changing your mind does not mean you have failed. There are alternatives."

"I know, and you're correct."

"What have you decided?"

"I will value all that you teach me, hunting, shooting and gathering herbs, and how to start a fire without a flint."

Lance nodded and smiled. "You already know those skills; you just require more practice. Although, I'm dreadfully worried about the flint, that might be beyond your capabilities."

I punched his arm and followed him outside.

The rest of the day, we scrubbed the floors, cupboards, and the walls, then cleaned the windows. We worked on the shed, and Lance scoured the outdoor toilet with boiling water. While I was preparing supper, he chopped more wood and started a reserve pile next to the campfire.

I reheated the leftovers and used some of the food we took from Pete's root cellar. I fried potatoes and set out raw carrots, and we each had half an apple for dessert. There was still some pemmican left, and the dried beans and chestnuts.

Later, we went outside and sat on the porch. We discussed the issue of wildfires and the damage done to our forests and streams. Then our conversation turned to environmental and climate change. Lance was knowledgeable in those areas, and he pointed out it was impractical that man ignore wildfire and extreme flooding; seeking new skills and knowledge not only provided the tools necessary to navigate unforeseen challenges; it also equipped us to adapt. Resource decline and ecological degradation were major world concerns.

"Reduce, reuse and recycle" Lance murmured.

I listened closely, "How is it you know so much about these matters?"

He stretched his back and shoulders and leaned against the edge of the table. "The Similkameen and Chinese residents of Blackfoot share their cultures, traditions, and specific requirements with each other. They do this by interacting with our students, parents and community members through stories, traditions, and languages."

"Sounds ideal," I whispered.

"It can be," Lance answered. "Still, it takes extreme effort and determination."

We sat quietly, enjoying the warmth radiating from the stove.

I did not know what lay ahead, and having Lance around lessened my anxiety. I understood he would not stay long, I must learn what he was willing to teach and share.

Chapter Eleven

My training began immediately. Lance took me with him when he went big game hunting and was impressed when he pointed at an animal track and I guessed correctly. We dressed the deer, packed the meat in Lance's tarp, and secured it to Ringo's back. We arrived back at the cabin at dusk. I recalled the time Taylor, and I trapped and stalked big game, without the luxury of a pack horse.

We worked on my shooting as often as we could, and I gradually improved. I mentioned the instructions I got from Taylor, and when I got injured and couldn't fire a rifle and had to forego the lessons. Lance told me I would never be a sharpshooter, but if I could protect myself should the time come, then he would be satisfied with my progress.

I made a point of listening closely to his instructions, and if I made a mistake, he was patient with me.

The weather turned warmer, and summer arrived. We rode south along the Tulameen River to Podunk Creek, or west towards the Forest Service Road. Mount

Tulameen was visible in the distance, and I asked Lance if we could stop as I wanted to make a quick sketch as I aimed to paint it when we got back to the cabin. He mentioned the climb to the summit was challenging, though on the other hand, the scenery from the top was breathtaking. He thought I might be interested in viewing it one day.

I told Lance about our trek to the Interior, hauling three young children and carrying heavy backpacks all the way, climbing mountains, fording streams and hiking across the Wastelands, and decided I had done enough travelling for the time being. Lance chuckled and told me he understood how I felt.

On one of our hikes, Lance took me to the Upper Similkameen River Valley, and we eventually arrived at the Tulameen Ochre Cliffs. We rode along a path, he halted Ginger, then turned and faced me.

"This is the Spirit Trail, and it has spirit power, Tulameen means "red earth.""

"I know, it's the rock dust used to make ochre."

Lance raised his eyebrows in surprise. "This is the route our group took on our trek to Princeton," I grinned. "Mai-Li told us about the rock paintings and showed them to us."

Lance dismounted and removed a small metal pail from his backpack. He filled it with red earth and informed me when we returned to the cabin, he would show me the process of changing it into paint.

Frequently, I paused to sketch flowers, herbs, trees, and plants, and occasionally, we stumbled across deserted homesteads. I made quick sketches, which I drew and painted when we got back to the cabin. I was infatuated by the earthy tones that complemented the brown, rust, and olive-green colours of the log cabins and barns.

I recalled Taylor sharing his desire to preserve the histories of the deserted towns and mines. I wondered if he found what he was looking for while he travelled with Pete. I was gradually coming to terms with our separation and hoped one day I would come to terms regarding our feelings for each other.

The days became warmer and milder, there was an abundance of berries, foliage, and herbs. Lance shared a wealth of information about them, and I started a notebook and wrote the material down; it would be invaluable to have when I was on my own.

He showed me how to make moccasins from deer hide, and I told him Mai-Li helped me make a pair.

He pointed at my feet. "Are those the moccasins you made?"

I nodded happily and lifted my foot to show him my handiwork.

"It's a good thing Mai-Li has so much patience," he muttered before he opened the cabin door and escaped.

Days later, after eating a late supper, we went outside and sat on the porch steps. It was peaceful, crickets chirped, and an owl hooted in a nearby tree, softening the mood. Lance took my hand, then turned and faced me. "Carlie, I find myself caring about you more deeply than I thought I would."

I twitched, then pulled back my hand. "Lance, I'm sorry, I don't know if I feel the same way about you."

"Are you saying there's not the slightest chance you might change your mind?"

"No, of course not... I fell in love with Taylor, and he denied his support, then he deserted me and left me on my own. At this time, it would be premature to consider anyone else, particularly given the current circumstances."

"Carlie, I'm not Taylor."

"I know, however, for now I must find my place in this world, and I can't do that if I rely on another person. Does that make sense?"

"Yes, it does," Lance sighed. "I won't bring this matter up again, and when you finally decide what you want, let me know."

"I will, I promise."

Occasionally, Lance saddled Ginger and disappeared. I assumed he wanted time alone, as spending hours with a greenhorn was wearing him down. He often returned carrying herbs and berries, and I wondered why he did not invite me to join him.

Late one afternoon when he returned from another outing, I shadowed him inside the cabin and cleared my throat, catching his attention. He was carrying a bag of moss and roots which he placed on the table. He turned and looked at me.

"What do you do all day?"

"Mostly ride," he answered, "Why do you ask?"

"You're gone all the time, and sometimes you return carrying nothing. Am I driving you crazy?"

Lance chuckled and shook his head. "No, you're not, I can cover more ground when I'm alone."

"Are you looking for something?"

"Where the larger animals graze, which makes it easier to track them when we are low on meat."

I knew there was more, so I waited for him to continue. "You mentioned you and Taylor found a yew tree close by, I wouldn't mind if you showed me where it's located, my supply of arrows is low, and I need to replace them."

All the while Lance spoke, he did not look directly at me, he strolled to the back window and stared outside. I knew he was not being completely honest with me.

"Never mind," I mumbled. "You're not obliged to answer, it's none of my business."

"Whoa, where did that come from?"

"I know when you are lying to me, Lance. I will try harder to learn, and I'll do more around the cabin."

Lance exhaled, took my hand, and led me to the table. He gestured me to sit, then sat down next to me. "That is not the reason I've been scrutinizing the area. Ever since we talked about Lars, I can't get him out of my mind. He might come here, so it is necessary we stay diligent and alert."

"I should never have mentioned him; the chances of Lars finding the cabin are remote. Not only is he a coward but he would not be interested in you; he's determined to find Taylor and would not challenge you."

"That's not what's worrying me, Carlie. If he finds you, he will know Taylor is somewhere in the vicinity and would use you as leverage. If that man is angry enough to search for Taylor, he is not going to worry about me. Taylor knows how to take care of himself; he is proficient in weaponry and fighting, but Lars also knows Taylor's weak spot, and that's you."

"Lars is angry and bitter, and obsessed with finding Taylor," I added. "I imagine the Desert Rats got tired of his leadership, and it would not surprise me if they ordered him to leave. He won't try to find Taylor on his own, he was brave when his gang backed him, I imagine he'll find some lowlife he can bully and force into helping him."

"That doesn't make me feel any better. I'll stop looking if you promise to stay close to the cabin and not wander off on your own. Make sure I'm with you all the time. Is that a deal?"

"Yes, of course."

"Thank you."

"I'm going to paint; I hope to finish the one I started yesterday of the wild mushrooms. I'm having trouble with the colours."

"You'll figure it out, and while you're doing that, I'm going to read my book."

It was silent and pleasant in the cabin. When it got darker, Lance lit the propane lantern, and I worked another hour, then called it a night.

I got my pyjamas and dressed in the shed. Lance, on the other hand, suffered no inhibitions about undressing in the cabin.

I raced across the cabin floor, got into my bag, then turned and faced the wall.

Night Carlie."

"Night Lance."

Chapter Twelve

The days passed quickly, there was never a shortage of work. We cleaned, chopped, and stacked wood, and when the pantry was packed with herbs, roots, and berries, I felt more comfortable.

Late one afternoon, Lance handed me a sheet of paper and instructed me to write down in numbered paragraphs information he wanted to share to help me survive on my own. I sat down, nervously chewing the end of my pencil.

He stood, paced the floor, muttered in Nsyilxcən, then joined me at the table.

No. 1: The stream behind the cabin has cold, clear water, which should be boiled before drinking. (I reminded him I was aware of this as in today's world a person would be foolhardy to drink water directly from any lake or stream. He told me to pay attention and not interrupt).

No. 2: Start a garden to grow crops of the local vegetation. Make sure it was not situated under the trees as it would require direct sunlight. He suggested I locate it at the bottom of the hill in the back yard, next to the stream (I wrote and nodded, wondering where I would find a shovel to dig the garden). At this point, he handed me a wooden box filled with bags of seeds: tomatoes, carrots, potatoes, peas, beans, and an instruction sheet on how to plant and grow them.

No. 3: Start a compost made up of waste and rubbish. This would make excellent fertilizer for the garden. (The first thing that came to mind were the bears, wolves, and cougars, attracted to the scent of decay. I prayed he would leave enough ammunition).

No. 4: Then staring directly at me and sighing heavily, he told me I must have a first aid kit. He intended to leave bandages and pain killers in the event I needed them in the event of an emergency. The look on his face was not reassuring. (I thanked him and realized it would not be prudent for me to deduce what would happen if I were attacked by a bear, wolf, or cougar and the only First Aid I had was a box of bandages and a handful of pain killers, but I wisely kept that idea to myself)

No. 5: Then he questioned me about my snowshoes, and I sheepishly told him I forgot to pack them. I imagine by now he was ready to pull out his hair. (this one I realized was my own stupid mistake, although at the time I left Blackfoot, I carried a full backpack and my rifle).

There was silence in the room. I scanned through my notes, turned, and looked at Lance. "I'm really in trouble, aren't I?"

"Not if you pay attention, you should be fine. If it is more than you can manage, you can always change your mind and leave."

"I wouldn't get far; I have too much to carry."

"You won't have to do that; I propose to leave Thunder with you. I'll make sure he listens to you, which means it's necessary you do more riding before I leave."

"'Even if I decided to leave, I don't think I can remember the route we took through the forest."

"Thunder knows, just tell him to go home. By the time you arrive at Blackfoot Road, you can head north or south, by then you should have decided your destination."

"Lance, you know I cannot return to Blackfoot, I will not be welcome there. That leaves Princeton, and after what you told me about it, I would be crazy to go there."

"You know I won't be leaving until I know you can cope on your own. As well, I plan to return periodically to check on you."

"You have enough to do when you return home; you don't need to babysit me."

"Let's not worry about that, we have a lot to do before then."

The rest of the week we spent digging and planting the garden following Lance's mother's instructions she had packed with the seeds. (I was not surprised when Lance dug a shovel out of his supplies). Then he dug a compost pit, and I gathered grass, leaves, yard waste, and kitchen scraps. He explained the process to me, which I added to my list of numbered paragraphs:

No. 6: Compost - wait a couple of months. In the meantime, check it daily to see if it is ready, put your hand in the middle of the pile; if it's warmer than the surface, do not turn it. When it's time to use the compost, scoop it from the bottom. (by now my stomach was heaving and I was not sure if I really wanted, or for that matter, was prepared to plant a garden)

We continued to explore the surrounding area, and I spent hours sketching and writing descriptions of the wildflowers, plants, and trees. Lance took me to several abandoned ghost towns. We stopped at Granite Creek, and I sat on the ground and stared at the dilapidated cabins, recalling the time our group stopped here on our way to the Interior.

Lance sat down next to me. "Carlie, is something wrong?"

I shook my head and decided the last thing he wanted to hear was me reminiscing about Taylor and his dreams.

"It's nothing, I was just wondering about the people who settled here, whether they prospered and felt fortunate, and why they left."

"At times, life was gruelling back then; most of the resident's mined gold or coal, and when the mines dried up, they moved on.”

“Yet people are once again returning to the land, do you believe they will be successful?”

“If they develop personal relationships with the land and interact with the environment, not destroy it. The only way they can do that is live in harmony with nature.”

“There has to be more to it than that; will they be able to survive, earn a living and support their families?”

“It will be a learning process, and that is the reason we have community get-togethers where people can voice their opinions and concepts. We instruct our children about food and medicine collected from the land, take them on ecological trips, visit archaeological sites to gain knowledge about their ancestors, and explore the night sky from an Indigenous perspective.”

“Do the Chinese have the same views?”

“They have their own beliefs, similar to the Similkameen, and we have learned to exist in harmony.”

“Does that mean Blackfoot will expand, or are the residents prepared to move to remote areas?”

“It will not grow more in size, the plan is to rebuild the vacant towns such as Granite Creek, Coalmont, Blakeburn, and Allenby. Many of our residents have shown interest, and Blackfoot’s success proves that it is possible. We have expanded our meetings and ideas to include the locals of Princeton who might also be interested."

"Maybe one day a family will move to the cabin full time, it's located in a perfect spot, there's plenty of water close by, and game animals are abundant." I muttered to myself.

"Do you intend to have a family one day?" Lance probed.

"One day, I suppose, if I find the right person."

"Don't look too far, he might be closer than you think."

My face turned red, and I returned to my drawing. I realized my life was at a crossroads, but I had no idea what I sought after and where I aimed to go. I was frustrated and angry all the time. Had I made the right decision to live on my own? I missed Eddie daily, we were meant to be a family, although prior to returning to him, it was essential I made some important decisions. I realized I still longed for Taylor, and it was time to let him go. Lance was a thoughtful, intelligent man, and he admitted he loved me, and in time, I would be able to return my sentiments. He made me laugh, feel safe, and I think about him more than I should.

I understood my artistic abilities would become a prominent part of my life, and living on my own with nature felt genuine. Was I headed in the correct direction, and although I did not know what lay ahead, I hoped I would find the strength to acquire what I sought.

Chapter Thirteen

As Lance promised, I resumed my riding lessons, at times frustrated beyond reason when Thunder rejected my commands.

"Carlie, you must be more assertive...."

"I know, I know, show him who's boss." I answered sharply.

Lance shook his head and patiently explained the last step again.

"I can't do it," I yelled in frustration.

"Yes, you can, you're as stubborn as he is, quit competing with him."

"You like him better than me," I muttered, as I rode past Lance.

"Right now, that is definitely true," he grumbled.

I twisted in the saddle and glared at him. At that moment, I decided I did not want the hassle of learning to ride, or having a horse, I could manage on my own.

"Can we stop now?" I vented angrily as I pulled back on Thunder's reins to stop him from heading to the creek.

The look on Lance's face was answer enough. "For now," he answered curtly, clenching his teeth. "First thing in the morning, we start where we left off."

I dismounted, forgetting how tall Thunder was. Lance snatched me before I face-planted on the ground. I followed him into the cabin, poured water into the basin, and washed my hands and face. It was a long, tiring day, and I wanted to work on my latest drawing.

"What's for supper, I'm starved?"

I turned and faced Lance. "Aren't we finishing the quail," I stammered, suddenly aware of how late it was.

Lance wandered into the shed and returned with potatoes, herbs, and a fish he caught yesterday in the stream. He laid the food on the counter, then found his book and settled comfortably on his bed. Quail was unquestionably off the menu tonight, and he knew how much I hated scaling and cleaning fish. I peeled the potatoes, poured water into the pot, and put it on the back burner. I rummaged around until I found the frying pan and slammed it down on the stove surface.

"Save the peelings for the compost," Lance reminded me without lifting his head.

Oh, he was good! Retribution at its finest.

We ate in silence, the fish was delicious, still I refused to award him the satisfaction of sharing that with him. After I washed the dishes, I sat at the table and worked on my latest artwork. Time passed, and the golden rays of the setting sun cast a warm glow on the cottage walls. Stiffly, I stood and stretched my arms and back and turned sharply when I sensed Lance standing behind me.

"You scared me," I gasped.

"Sorry, you were so focused, I didn't mean to disturb you. It's an idyllic night, why don't we sit on the porch."

I shrugged, sat down, and picked up my paint brush.

"Carlie, I'm sorry I took my anger out on you," he said, breaking the stillness. "I've never trained anyone who's not familiar with or never ridden a horse, and I must confess, there are times when I get frustrated."

"Because I'm slow to learn, and I'm afraid of horses?" I stated.

"You definitely are not slow to learn, you do, however, have a fear of horses, but hopefully that will pass in time."

A full moon cast a radiant glow through the cabin window. "It's a full moon, why don't we take advantage of it," Lance said, reaching for my hand.

I hesitated, then cleaned my paintbrush and stood. I followed him outside and sat on the porch step. The moonlight created a soft light around the treetops. I pointed at a shooting star streaking across the night sky. Lance turned his focus on the horses grazing near the tree line. He stayed silent, deep in reflection.

"Let's form a truce," he declared, turning to look at me. "If you consider I'm overly impatient or pressuring, let me know, it's just that in our band, the majority learned to be skilled riders before they knew how to walk."

"I know you're looking out for me," I whispered. "And I also know once you deem it's time to return to Blackfoot, you'll leave."

"That is the plan, I believe."

"I don't want you to go," I blurted.

I lowered my face, afraid to look into his eyes, I had no idea why I told him that.

He turned and faced me, then he leaned towards me, lifted my chin, and kissed me lightly.

"Finally, we're on the same page," he whispered.

I pulled back at a loss for words. Why were my memories so irrational? Inside I was confused and scared. I stared at him, we moved our bodies closer, and he caressed my shoulders. He smiled and kissed me again.

"I've longed to do that for a long time," he admitted.

"I know."

"Carlie, you're sending me mixed signals, it is crucial you disclose what you've decided to do. Are you planning to stay here at the cabin on your own?"

I lowered my head, then shrugged my shoulders. Lance waited patiently for me to answer.

"I don't know, I thought if I survived on my own, I would be able to face challenges and not rely all the time on others."

"You are no different than anyone else our age. It is the reason the First Nations people partake in Spirit Quests. We learn survival skills, how to connect with nature, and how to be more independent and self-reliant."

"I sense my life has no direction," I admitted. "It is necessary I discover a purpose in my life, and I don't know where to start."

"Those emotions are normal, and often vary, depending on an individual's personal experiences."

"I suppose that is why I'm so disoriented. Losing my family, struggling to survive on my own for two years, experiencing Rusty's death, and then losing Taylor, it all seems hopeless to me."

"When the time is right, you'll find your way and recognize what path to take."

"What if it never happens?"

"It will, I have something to tell you, please listen to me before you react."

I stiffened and experienced a sense of foreboding.

"Carlie, I had originally intended on returning to Blackfoot. When you told me about Lars, concerns involving him showing up have been haunting me, and when you admitted you intended to stay, I decided not to go."

"No, Lance, I can't let you do that," I exclaimed, shaking my head frantically. I stood and headed towards the cabin. Lance reached up and grabbed my arm.

"Carlie, wait a minute."

"I will not let you alter your plans," I declared, twisting to face him. "The residents in Blackfoot are expecting you to return."

"That decision is mine, and mine alone. I've told you this before."

"If you stay, all it proves is that I'm a failure, that I can't cope on my own."

"Asking assistance takes courage in recognizing you demand support. Relying on others is a normal part of life."

"What if I don't succeed, then I'll just be plain, hopeless Carlie."

Lance smiled. "First, you are not plain or hopeless by a long shot, and secondly, you're far too stubborn to fail."

"I'm not plain," I pondered.

"That's what you got out of what I just said." Lance sighed.

Then he reached behind me and opened the cabin door.

Chapter Fourteen

The next couple of days, we gardened, hunted, and fished. Then I took Lance to the yew tree, and he cut off stems and limbs and made a new batch of arrows. Then he decided I should learn how to shoot them, although I reminded him Taylor had tried before, and at that time I was declared a hopeless cause. After a gruelling afternoon he came to the same conclusion and decided to find something easier for me to tackle. I never let him know how relieved I was when he made that decision.

"You mentioned there was a willow bush not far from here," he queried. "We need more rope, and we might as well start working on snowshoes."

"Just how long are we staying here?" I questioned.

"As long as it takes. If we have an early winter, and the snow is deep, the horses will have difficulty getting around. The canyons and gullies are steep and slippery, and I cannot take a chance one of them will fall and break a leg. The snowshoes work better in deep snow."

I nodded and mentioned the time Taylor and I had gone hunting and tracked down a yearling moose. Taylor killed it with an arrow, as he always saved his ammunition for emergencies. Lance nodded and seemed uninterested in discussing the experiences Taylor and I shared. I imagine he wondered if I still had feelings for Taylor.

Time passed peacefully, and we often ventured deep into the surrounding forest, discovering abandoned, forgotten homesteads. We returned to Granite Creek, and Lance talked about its history. At one time there were more than two hundred buildings in the town, thirteen saloons, and by 1885, two thousand people lived there. The miners found platinum and gold in the creeks, although many of them did not realize the value of platinum until later. When the town was deserted, a few hopeful miners remained. I sketched the dilapidated cabins and barns, wondering about the people who existed there, and what happened to them after they left.

Days later, Lance wondered if I would be interested in going to the Tulameen Falls, which was located about thirty kilometres north of our location. He explained the depth of the falls was 1400 feet and thought I might be interested in sketching and painting it.

"That's a great idea; how long will it take us to arrive there?"

"If we leave early enough, the horses could make it in one day. Because of wildfires and climate changes, many of the hiking trails in the Interior have not been maintained, and there's a chance the trail to the falls is in poor shape." Lance reasoned aloud. "It's been a while since I've been there; however, I do remember it being steep, rugged and surrounded by old forest."

"Although it sounds fascinating, are you sure it's safe to go there? What about the garden; doesn't it have to be watered while we're gone?"

"Okay, Worrywart, I'll try and rig something up, maybe a drip irrigation system using the water from the stream."

I nodded, pretending I knew what he was talking about.

I weeded and watered the garden, while Lance explained the irrigation system he assembled, it was rudimentary and simple, according to him. He angled a barrel next to the stream, where water would leisurely seep into, then trickle down to the garden through rivulets.

That night after we ate, Lance took a sheet of paper and drew a map showing the route we would be taking. He explained that travelling northeast and following the Tulameen River to the falls would take longer as we had to ride through heavily forested areas which would slow our progress. Trusting his knowledge of the surrounding area, he decided we would head northwest towards Vuich Creek.

Before retiring for the night, Lance instructed me to pack enough clothing and food to last for four days. He reminded not to forget my rifle, as we would be riding on remote trails and in uninhabited areas. He would ride Ginger, I Thunder, while Ringo carried the supplies. I hoped my riding lessons would come in handy, as the notion of Thunder misbehaving made me nervous, especially if we encountered a bear or a cougar.

Early the next morning, I wrapped all the perishable food in one of the cloth bags Mai-Li and I had left in the cabin. We saddled the horses and fastened the supplies on Ringo. I glanced at the cabin one last time as I steered Thunder into the trees.

We rode most of the morning and eventually arrived at the convergence of Vuich Creek and the Tulameen River Forest Service Road. The river was running high, and Lance crossed first with Ginger and Ringo and when they reached the far side, he signalled me to follow.

I steered Thunder into the water and dredged up memories of the hours Lance spent training me and the high-strung horse. I gave Thunder free-rein, and he headed straight towards his friends. Lance smiled when we arrived, and I imagine he was relieved I made it across the creek without any mishap. I trailed him as he guided Ginger and Ringo into the dense underbrush, and we soon arrived at the road.

It twisted and turned and at times we lost sight of Vuich Creek.

We rode at a steady pace, and when Lance got too far ahead, he stopped Ginger and waited until Thunder caught up. Lance leaned forward and stretched. "I think we'll spend the night at Sutter Creek, it's an open recreation site sheltered and located on the high banks of the creek."

We eventually arrived at our destination; mountains rose majestically in the background, offering awe-inspiring vistas, supporting unique flora and fauna. I told Lance I was dying to make sketches of the surrounding area, and he grinned.

"First, let's set up camp, and have something to eat."

"I'll need the light to draw so can you make supper," I murmured, keeping my head down. I figured it was worth a try.

"Anything to get out of cooking," Lance chuckled.

I inhaled sharply, as I experienced an unnerving sensation of déjà vu; suddenly Mai-Li's face came into focus, and I remembered her saying the same thing when I tried the same tactic on her. I shook my head in frustration, why couldn't I stop deliberating about my past?

Lance must have noticed the alteration in my manner, yet he remained silent. We found a location to set up the tent, then I found my artbook and pencils, and sat near the edge of the bank that offered a clear view where Sutter Creek merged with Vuich Creek. I propped my binder against my knees and pencilled the landscape.

I lost track of time and jumped when a shadow blocked the light of the sun. Lance was standing over me carrying a plate of food.

"Your meal, your highness," he proclaimed, bowing deeply.

I giggled and set aside my drawing. I rose and reached for the plate. He raised it above his head and out of reach. "I've been cooking all afternoon, and I deserve a kiss, or two."

"Hey, that's blackmail," I exclaimed.

"Depends how hungry you are," he smirked.

I sighed, kissed him, and took the plate.

That was when I discovered Lance was an excellent cook, something at which I was not proficient. I had to figure a way to get him to do all the cooking, whether we were camping or back at the cabin.

"This is really good," I mumbled, in between bites. "You should take over the cooking, Lance."

He snorted, finished eating, and handed me the plate. Message received!

While I cleaned the dishes, Lance took the horses down to the creek for a drink, then let them graze. There was plenty of grass, bushes, dandelions, and clover. He showed me how to groom them properly by picking their hooves, using a curry comb on their bodies, checking for injuries, combing their tails, and inspecting their eyes and noses. I respected his concern over the well-being of his horses.

We sat around the campfire and welcomed the silence. Lance drew me close then placed his arm around my shoulder. There was a full moon, and the moonlight glinted off the water, creating a silver path; the trees and leaves shimmered with a silver glow, and the chirping of crickets added a peaceful ambience.

"It's late," Lance announced. "We'll wake up early, it's a brief ride to the Vuich Falls Recreation Site from here, and we can stop there to eat before we go to the falls. There's a nearby trail with views of the surging waters of the creek; we'll skip that right now. We can do it another time."

"Your wish is my command, oh mighty leader," I replied.

"As long as you know whose boss," he snickered.

"Keep that up, and you're cooking supper again tomorrow!"

"Hmm, where was I. Oh yeah, the trail that leads to the falls is located at the Tulameen River and the Vuich Creek crossings."

"Are they manageable to cross?" I inquired.

Lance poured water on the campfire and checked to make sure the embers were completely out. "Yes, we're still in high water season, so it's imperative we stay alert and are careful where we go. It's close to the falls, no more than a kilometre. The trail is steep with an easy tread, and twists through an old forest. We'll pass jagged rock bluffs along the river's edge. A person can reach the falls in twenty minutes. Right now, I'm not sure of the current condition of the pathway, and I prefer not to take any chances. We'll ride at a leisurely pace, it's safer for us and the horses."

"What's it like at the falls," I asked.

"There's camping there, but it's rustic. They allow small fires; we'll use the fire rings."

"What's a fire ring?"

Lance turned and looked at me, shaking his head. "So much to learn and so little time," he muttered.

I laughed and waited for his response. "It's a container or a structure, circular, made of stone, metal or brick and set up on dirt or sand. It's safer than an open fire and catches sparks and stops fires from spreading."

"Oh, that makes sense," I reasoned.

"It does. I forgot to mention we can swim in the pool or take a shower in the fall's mist, if you're interested."

"Swim, shower?" I spluttered.

"You do know how to swim, don't you?"

"I grew up in Vancouver near the Pacific Ocean; I was swimming before I was walking."

"Excellent," Lance acknowledged. "Have you ever skinny dipped?"

I swallowed, and felt my face turn red.

How are you going to talk your way out of this one Carlie?

Chapter Fifteen

We woke early, ate a quick breakfast, and fed the horses. We were on the trail when the sun appeared on the horizon, casting a warm golden glow over the treetops. After a short ride, we arrived at the crossings. We shadowed the bluff and guided the horses through loose rocks and rubble. Turning a corner on the path, Lance stopped Ginger and Ringo, then turned and motioned me to dismount. A massive cedar branch was lying across the trail, blocking our progress.

"Is there room to go around?" I queried.

Lance grinned, untied the pannier, and removed his axe. He chopped, while I stood to the side and observed a pileated woodpecker pound on a nearby cedar, marking its territory and feeding on insects.

It was not long before Lance finished splitting the branches, I helped him remove the chopped limbs from the pathway.

"At one time in the past, I imagine heavy rains increased the flow of the falls, which caused the stream to flood and damage part of the trail," he guessed. "Adding climate change and wildfires to the list is reason enough to keep most people away from here.”

“Should we go any farther,” I asked anxiously.

“We’re almost to the top, let’s keep going and have a look around.”

We remounted and continued our climb. It was not long until we reached our destination; I overheard the roar of the waterfall before I saw it. The horses balked and Lance gestured me to dismount. Then he tied Ringo to a tree and left Ginger and Thunder to free graze.

I stayed close to Lance as we approached the falls. Clear water tumbled down rocky cliffs, and a cool spray of mist covered my face. I breathed in the scent of damp earth and moss. Gushing water landed in a pool beneath the falls, creating eddies and swirls.

“Lance, it’s magnificent, everything is so lush.”

Lance scooped water into his cupped hands. “Water supports all life,” he whispered. “We must protect and conserve it for generations to come.”

“That’s inspiring advice,” I whispered humbly.

“Water holds significant cultural and spiritual meaning for Indigenous people. It is a living entity with its own spirit, and it is our responsibility to protect and care for it.”

“Thanks for sharing that with me, Lance.”

He nodded, then pointed to a flat piece of land on the far side of the pool. "That's a reasonable location for the tent; let's start a campfire; we're almost out of water."

I paced behind Lance down the trail to retrieve the horses. I took Thunder's reins and followed Lance, Ginger, and Ringo to the falls. When we arrived, Ringo bolted, and Lance calmed the jumpy horse. Then we headed to the campsite. After we removed the tack and supplies, we led them to the edge of the pool and allowed them to drink.

As we returned to the campsite, Lance mentioned. "I'm going to highline all three of the horses tonight, there might be bears in the area."

"What's a highline?" I asked.

"I figured you'd quiz me," Lance laughed. "It's a way to protect not only the horses and our environment; it causes less damage to tree bark and their root systems."

"What a splendid idea," I remarked.

Lance grinned, and I followed him back to where we left the supplies. "Now pay attention to the instructions, there WILL be a test later."

I smirked and shrugged my shoulders.

He removed a leather bag and unzipped it.

"This is a tree saver strap," he began, removing one article at a time. "This is a nylon rope, and here are two no-knot swivel line ties." Then he lifted the leather bag and started lecturing. "This is a zipped nylon storage bag to keep articles in, which allows effortless packing and transport."

I stifled a yawn and pretended I was interested. "Thank you, I don't know how I'd survive without this valuable information."

"Next, I will show you how to set up the highline, how to tie the ropes properly, then..."

"Oh dear," I interrupted. "I really must leave, I have a tent to install, and kindling to gather, you're on your own."

Setting up the tent was not one of my favourite jobs, however learning the names of each individual piece of the highline and how to install it was about as thrilling as digging for worms.

Lance completed the highline, I was half-way through setting up the tent when he joined me. With his help, we soon finished, and then we hauled our supplies and bedrolls inside.

"You hungry?" he asked.

"Starving."

Lance dug out the leftover pancakes from breakfast and handed one to me and kept two for himself. "This should tide us over until supper. You can start working on your sketches if you wish. In the meantime, I am going to have a look around. Keep your rifle nearby; there could be bears or cougars in the area. It was evident climbing the trail, there was little traffic coming to the falls; it would make a good watering hole for wildlife."

Lance salvaged his bow and arrow from the tent, I waved goodbye, absorbed in trying to capture the flow of the water, eddies and whirlpools. I did not pick up a sound until he approached me and leaned over my shoulder.

"Nice," he complimented. "That's an impressive landscape you've captured."

I gasped and spun around, my pulse racing. "Lance, don't do that, you almost gave me a heart attack."

"I've been gone for a while, you have any visitors," he queried abruptly.

I shook my head and looked away.

"What if a bear or a cougar was in the area" he persisted. "You wouldn't have heard a thing until it was too late."

Then he looked intently at me, and he was not smiling. "By the way, where's your rifle?"

I closed by artbook, turned and pointed towards the tent.

"Carlie, you must be diligent at all times when you're alone in the wilderness, I can't stress that enough."

I did not answer, realizing there was no excuse for my carelessness.

"With your history, I'd assume you'd be more cautious."

"What do you mean by that."

"I understand wild cats in particular are attracted to you."

"Who told you that?"

"Taylor. We talked about your journey to the interior, and he mentioned you had a few close encounters."

"That information is private; he should not have mentioned it."

"He also mentioned your confrontation with Willie."

I jerked, took a deep breath, and closed my eyes. Noticing my reaction, Lance reached over and took my hand.

"Carlie, he didn't provide any details and I didn't probe. He brought it up as he blamed himself for not being more cautious; he was aware Willie threatened to retaliate when he was banished from the cabin for stealing food."

Upset and embarrassed, I looked at Lance. "Why did you bring this up?" I cried. "I don't want to discuss Taylor or Willie again, as far as I'm concerned neither of them exist."

Then I stood, ran into the tent, and angrily pulled down the flap.

I sat on my camp bag; took a deep breath and covered my mouth with my hands. Why was I so upset with Lance; he was only trying to protect me. I should have paid attention and taken the time to retrieve my rifle. He had every right to be irate; I was the one who was negligent.

I perceived movement outside the tent, then Lance entered and sat down next to me. I was not prepared to speak with him; I lay back and pulled my bedroll over my head.

Was I being overly sensitive, afraid of sharing personal information? Was that one of the reasons I was reluctant to commit to a new relationship, why I pushed Lance away when he made advances, or tried to be intimate?

"Carlie, I'm sorry." Lance whispered. "Can we talk about it; I shouldn't have used them as an example; I wanted you to understand the graveness of being negligent in the wilderness."

I closed my eyes, and Taylor came to mind. Was I focusing on him because he shared personal information with Lance, information I preferred to leave buried.

I lowered my bag and looked at Lance. He was sitting cross-legged on the floor, and he reached over and took me in his arms. It was then I realized I was crying.

"Lance," I stammered "I'm sorry I reacted the way I did, and being reminded of Taylor and Willie, made me realize it's too soon to put the past behind me and move on with my life. I hope you can understand."

"Carlie, you do not need to apologize, I should not have mentioned either of them. I was angry because you disregarded my instructions and put yourself in danger, but I'm more annoyed I left you on your own. I would never forgive myself if anything happened to you."

"I guess I'm not as skilled in wilderness survival as I believed."

"No, you are not, which is one of the reasons I've decided to stay longer at the cabin. Are you comfortable with that?"

"I guess so. What's the other reason you're staying?"

Lance lowered his head, smiled and looked into my eyes. "Because you have feelings for me, you may not know it yet, but you will."

I lay my head on his chest and closed my eyes.

"Carlie, from now on, if you ever want to talk, I promise to be there for you, to listen, and not bring up emotional wounds."

"Thanks Lance, I'll take you up on that."

"Let's get something to eat, then later we'll swim in the pool."

"In...in the pool. Do I have to?"

"No, of course not, you can keep your clothes on if you are more comfortable, they should dry before morning."

"Am I that obvious?"

"Oh yes!"

I raised my head and kissed him. Then I stood and lifted the tent flap. "Thanks Lance, I really appreciate your patience. I'll start supper."

"I suppose skinny dipping is off the agenda," he asked my retreating back.

I waved my hand in the air and left.

Chapter Sixteen

I woke with a start; Lance's bedroll was empty. I smiled remembering our swim in the pool last night. He joked and clowned around; his uncharacteristic behaviour surprised me as he was usually more serious and subdued. When he challenged me to a race around the pool, I was not far behind, and he nodded with approval.

I crawled from my bag and snatched my damp clothes; it would not take long before they dried. The aromatic aroma of freshly ground coffee drifted into the tent, and I dressed quickly and joined Lance at the fire.

"Is that coffee I smell?" I enquired.

"It is, you do know it'll stunt your growth," he warned as he filled my cup and handed it to me. "Never mind, it's too late, you're as tall as you're going to get."

I smirked and took a drink; the first sip of the day was by far the best.

"There's porridge and strawberries if you're hungry," he announced, pointing to a pot sitting on a rock next to the fire ring.

After we ate, I washed the dishes while Lance untied the horses and took them to the pool to drink, then he returned and tied them to the highline.

"Any ideas what to do today?" I asked, as I joined him.

"I was contemplating the Tulameen Ghost Town; you mentioned once you enjoyed drawing deserted homesteads and barns. After I considered it, and although it was tempting, I decided we would be too rushed. The round trip is more than sixty kilometres from here, and we're headed back to the cabin in a couple of days."

"Why is it called a ghost town, is it haunted?"

"People believe it is. There are three other deserted ghost towns besides Tulameen located on the Haunted BC Trail - Coalmont, Granite Creek, and Blakeburn; your group passed a few of them on your journey to the Interior. Of course, you're familiar with Blakeburn. Their historical stories are fascinating, unfortunately the round trip would take well over a week, and right now we do not have the time. The garden should be harvested, and there is work to be done around the cabin before the weather turns cold."

"You know," I whispered, not looking at Lance. "I don't believe in ghosts."

Lance raised his eyebrows and shook his head in disbelief. I'm sure I'll hear his views on that topic sometime soon.

"That would have been an amazing trip," I mentioned. "On our travels to the Interior our group passed the Granite Creek Cemetery, Taylor knew a lot about the town's history, however we didn't stop, the kids were tired, and we had a long hike ahead of us."

Lance nodded, and my reference to Granite Creek reopened a memory. "Taylor spoke about how he hoped one day to visit deserted towns and write about them, he felt it would preserve their histories. He also has an interest in discarded gold and silver mines."

"He discussed that with me," Lance added. "It would be valuable if he pursued his interest in those areas, although printing books might be difficult as Blackfoot does not have the means. He could preserve his manuscripts, research, artwork, and maps by donating them to the Blackfoot Library, we have archival collections to ensure the longevity of our historical, cultural, and administrative records. The information is available to all residents in Blackfoot and is taught in the schools as well."

"Maybe one day he will," I shrugged. Discussing Taylor and his aspirations brought back unwelcome memories.

"There are some hiking trails and streams in the area we haven't seen yet, and a scenic lookout behind the falls."

"I wouldn't mind working on more landscape scenes."

"Excellent, while you're doing that, I'll fish, the streams are ideal habitats for trout.

I can't think of a better way to spend an afternoon."

"Aren't we taking the horses?"

Lance shook his head. "Everything is within walking distance."

"What if a bear notices them."

"A bear would be mad to aggravate three grown horses; don't worry, if I considered they were in danger, I wouldn't leave them."

"Okay, you're the boss."

"It's about time you figured that out, woman," he muttered.

I snorted and followed Lance to the tent. I put my drawing equipment inside my backpack; Lance retrieved his bow and arrow.

We trudged down an overgrown path and arrived at a stream surrounded by trees and moss-covered rocks. Sunlight filtered through the mist created by the flowing water, creating a rainbow halo.

"Lance, look, there's a fish swimming in the shadows."

"Probably a trout or whitefish," he answered. "Both are good eating."

"While you're fishing, I'm going downstream to find an eddy or whirlpool created by water cascading over a rock."

"Oh, if that's all you want, lots of luck finding it," Lance commented.

I giggled and adjusted my backpack.

"Don't wander out of my sight, okay?" he warned.

"I won't."

I returned sooner than I intended.

"Let me guess, no whirlpools, cascading water, or huge boulders?" Lance remarked.

"Can we view the falls from the lookout?" I inquired.

"It's too rugged to climb from here, you can get there if you follow the trail from the Tulameen River Forest Service Road, which unfortunately is out of our way."

I nodded and turned to leave; Lance stopped me when he placed his hand on my arm.

"If we walk downstream, there's a beautiful open area, with a fantastic view of the mountain range, you want to give it a try?"

I followed Lance, and we soon arrived at a meadow, the scenery was spectacular. He lay nearby on the grass while I sketched. I discovered an unknown flower and when I asked him about it, he told me about its name in Similkameen, and said his people applied it as an herb in cooking. I was continually impressed with his knowledge of flora and fauna, and his passion about environmental causes and conservation.

"You're a Tree Hugger, aren't you?" I questioned.

"I've never been called that before?" Lance replied, lifting his head. "Is it an amazing thing, or a bad thing?"

I laughed. "It means you explore, study and observe nature all the time."

"I am inclined to do that, however, let's keep this a secret between ourselves, if anyone in Blackfoot discovers my new name, not only would I have to modify my calling, but I'd also have to move."

I laughed and folded my art book. "I'm finished here; do you want to return to the stream and fish a while?"

"I thought you'd never ask," Lance replied.

When we got back to the falls, I worked on a new drawing. I heard a splash behind me, Lance entered the shallow water, moved toward a big rock near a pile of sediment, reached underneath, pulled out his arm, and threw an enormous fish on the ground nearby. I jumped up and ran to where it landed.

"Wow," I exclaimed. "Can you show me how to do that?"

"Pay attention and watch how I do it."

It was not long when half a dozen fish met the same fate. I wanted to learn how to catch fish with my bare hands, since a stream flowed directly behind the cabin.

Late in the afternoon, fatigued and hungry, we returned to the falls. Lance warned me fish did not keep long and should be cleaned, scaled, and smoked immediately. He started a fire, and I sautéed two trout in the frying pan along with diced potatoes and herbs while Lance dealt with the scaling and cleaning.

Later, we swam in the pool, sat around the campfire, and drank coffee while I searched for satellites and falling stars.

The next morning, we ate a quick meal, packed, and left. I was pleased with the sketches I drew of the landscapes, trees, plants, flowers, birds, and even an annoying squirrel.

Late in the day, we arrived back at the cabin, Lance took care of the horses, and I hauled our supplies inside. I threw soiled clothing into the clothes basket, then hurried to the garden and checked on Lance's filter system. It had worked beautifully; the vegetables grew while we were gone; and it would not be long until we ate the lettuce and radishes.

Lance joined me at the garden and told me he checked around the cabin and found no signs of human or animal intruders.

Time passed productively, we kept busy working around the cabin. Lance weeded the garden, replenished our wood supply, did most of the cooking and hunted. I did the laundry, kept the cabin clean and orderly, and put aside a few hours each afternoon to work on my paintings.

When we ran low of herbs and edible plants, we took the gunny sack and one of Mai-Li's baskets and went foraging. I carried paper and a pencil with me and wrote down facts Lance shared about their culinary and medicinal benefits.

The days passed pleasantly, we were sitting on the porch steps, when Lance announced, he had decided to build a horse corral next to the cabin, the area was flat and shaded, and the water source was close. He worried about bears and cougars, if the horses panicked, they would run, and we could spend hours searching them. He was not as concerned about Ginger or Thunder as they were both trained to return to him; if Ringo spooked, he would be halfway home before Lance caught up to him. Over time, I came to appreciate how intelligent Ringo was, he just preferred carrying supplies not people.

Lance searched for fallen trees and salvaged the trunks, which he chopped into logs. He removed the bark and measured the length of the rails. I strolled down to Taylor's wood shop and found leftover nails, rope, and a hammer, which Lance used to secure the railings.

Days later, Lance advised that our food supply was low. We left early the next morning, and with the horses, covered twice as much ground in half the time as Taylor and I did when walking. I took him to the meadow where we found the moose, and we had not gone far when Lance spotted a deer on the far hillside. He gestured for me to dismount, then handed me Ringo's reins. He pointed to a dense thicket of brush, and I noiselessly led the two horses to the cover. I dismounted and squatted on the ground. I kept a firm grip on both reins as I did not want to give Thunder the opportunity to race after Ginger.

Lance rode into the heavy undergrowth and disappeared, carrying his bow and arrows. I did not wait long when I saw him on the trail. He galloped to where I was hidden.

"I've bagged a deer, but we have to butcher and pack it before it gets dark, I spotted cougar tracks close by, it's safer if we leave and not spend the night here."

I rode behind him to the kill; my stomach churned as I recalled how much I despised this chore. I reminded myself that the meat would provide food the rest of the summer and well into fall.

We field-dressed and cut the meat, then wrapped it in the tarp Ringo was carrying. By the time we packed the horses, it was late afternoon, the sun cast slanted shadows on the ground.

We rode for hours and reached the cabin at dusk, then we unpacked the horses and left the tarp on the porch. We took the horses to the corral and removed their equipment. While I filled their water trough and gave them oats, Lance took the tarp down to the creek and scrubbed it, then he flung it over a bush to let it dry before we stored it in the shed.

I started the stove and heated water, then Lance and I washed. I used the excess water to soak our clothes; tomorrow I would do laundry. Lance would smoke the deer meat, then I would help him after I finished doing the clothes.

Our days were busy and rewarding, Lance taught me how to start a fire without a flint. I hunted for ducks, grouse, rabbits, and yes even squirrels. Often, we packed a picnic, and explored neighbouring creeks with Ginger and Thunder, or discovered mysterious meadows secreted in mystical glens and valleys. I drew enough sketches to keep me occupied for the rest of the year.

There were times I sensed Lance watched me when I turned my back, his time to leave the cabin was rapidly approaching, and if I did not reveal my emotions to him, he would return to Blackfoot.

Time passed, and soon it was August. My nineteenth birthday was not far off, and I was no nearer to deciding where I wanted to be or what I intended to do with my life.

Late one afternoon, while sitting at the table discussing our next project at the cabin, Lance rose and approached me. He reached for my hand, pulled me up, and kissed me, when suddenly a current of cool air entered the room. I spun around and froze; Pete and Taylor were standing in the doorway.

Lance gently released me, then turned and calmly approached our unexpected guests. "Taylor, Grandfather, it is wonderful to see you, come in, you must be tired and hungry from your travels?"

Taylor moved aside as Pete entered the room, then he slammed the door. He turned sharply and glared angrily at me and Lance. "You want to tell me what the hell is going on?" he snarled.

Raw unspoken emotions resonated through the room. I stood rooted next to the table, my heart pounding.

Lance responded calmly. "We will have tea and eat, then we will have a discussion."

I went to the kitchen counter, poured water into the kettle, and placed it on the burner. My hands shook, my stomach knotted, an uncomfortable silence cloaked the room. I sluggishly entered the shed and returned with a plate of Bannock.

I nervously set the table; Taylor's eyes stalked me around the room. I kept my head lowered and avoided looking at him.

When the tea was steeped, I sat beside Lance while he poured. Pete reached over and took a Bannock.

"Carlie, this is delicious," he praised.

"I didn't make it, Lance did," I stammered. "I'm not very good at cooking."

I realized I was being disrespectful to Pete; however, found it challenging justifying his role in siding with Willie.

Lance conferred with his grandfather about his trip and listened respectfully as he shared his stories. Pete lit his pipe and smiled, how he could remain so passive was beyond me. Taylor remained silent; he drank a cup of tea but did not eat.

There was a lull in the conversation, and silence lingered in the room.

"Taylor," Lance began. "I will share what I know with you, but please don't interrupt until I have finished, if you do not wish to do so, then I would ask that you leave."

Taylor glared at the floor, then raised his head and countered. "I will respect your wishes."

Lance nodded, reached over, and took my hand. Taylor stiffened and remained silent.

"When you requested Carlie to pardon Willie, she refused to do so. You joined Grandfather when he left; she did not know you were gone. Mai-Li ordered her to confront and absolve Willie as well, again Carlie declined, and Mai-Li banned her and told her she must leave. Eddie was not allowed to accompany her. Grandfather was aware this might happen, and before he left, he asked me to keep an eye on Carlie, as he was concerned about her welfare. She was baffled, scared, and devastated in losing not only you, but Eddie as well. She originally planned to go to Princeton; I convinced her it was not safe for a young woman, or for that matter, any woman, to live there on her own. I persuaded her to allow me to accompany her to the cabin."

Pete remained silent while Lance spoke. Taylor was angry, and he focused on Lance. I placed my hand on Lance's arm to capture his attention. "Let me talk to him, please."

Lance hesitated, then agreed.

"Taylor," I mumbled, as my emotions tumbled over each other. Vivid memories returned; I took a deep breath and started again. "Taylor, without Lance I would not have survived. He taught me how to ride, when I was injured, he took care of me. He showed me how to plant a garden, and to make a compost heap. He showed me what herbs and roots were safe to eat, how to make Bannock and jerky, and smoked meat. He took me to several places where I could sketch the landscapes."

"Is that reason enough for you to be with him?" Taylor demanded sharply.

"You left me, you were not there when I needed support, and when I lost Eddie and was banned from Blackfoot, I had nowhere to go. I cannot forgive you leaving me on my own and not disclosing where you were going or when you expected to return. Mai-Li told me I must exonerate Willie, and if I did not, I would be expected to leave. I told her the same thing I told Pete; I cannot forgive or forget what he did to me. When I lost Eddie, it was as if I lost Rusty all over again."

The room became silent, and Taylor turned and stared out the window.

"I am sorry," I said quietly, "I do not care for you the same way I once did. I want someone I can rely on, someone who can accept me as I am. Your goals are so separate from mine, and know this, I will return to

Eddie and when I do, we will leave and start a new life, and you will never set eyes on either of us again."

Then I rose, Lance stood; I shook my head as I wanted to be alone. I wiped tears from my face and left the cabin.

Chapter Seventeen

I strolled to the corral and saw Pete's two horses, Lucy and Gus, at the water trough. Ringo spotted me and trotted over to the fence. Sensing I was unhappy, he playfully nipped my fingers. I turned when the sound of the cabin door opened. Taylor stood on the porch and monitored my movements. I could not read the expression on his face, anger I could deal with, pity I could not.

I left the corral, ambled to the creek, and headed upstream. I arrived at a flat boulder under an ancient lodgepole pine. The last time I was here, Willie threatened me at gunpoint, which prompted us to leave the cabin earlier than planned. Our small group eventually arrived at Blackfoot, naively expecting our ordeal was over.

The shock and grief of losing Taylor, coping with Pete's and Mai-Li's demands, and leaving Eddie behind left me empty. I picked up the sound of footsteps on the path and lifted my head, not surprised when Taylor approached me. He shuffled uneasily, unable to look at me.

"Carlie," he mumbled. "When Pete asked if I cared to join him on his expedition; I agreed. You and I quarrelled, and when I requested you communicate with Willie, you declined. You felt I took his side over yours, and you informed me you did not intend to see me again. I recognized we needed to spend time apart, or we would never reach a comparable agreement. When I said goodbye to Eddie and left him, I asked Mai-Li to let you know I was leaving. I assumed my message was passed on to you."

"What's done is done Taylor; whether I received your message or not was not the issue," I declared. "You knew I would not pardon Willie; you gave me an ultimatum and because of your betrayal, our relationship was over."

Taylor shook his head in denial; he did not dispute what I alleged.

"Twice, Mai-Li demanded I speak to Willie," I resumed. "And both times I said no. She then ordered me to leave. I asked her if you and Eddie would be going with me, and that was when she told me you left days before with Pete and assumed I knew. You had requested she take over Eddie's care; she was aware we were no longer together, and she told me I could not take him with me; he would stay with her."

"Carlie, I am so sorry what you suffered. Pete's offer to join him was an opportunity I couldn't pass, he had organized a small group to survey the abandoned mines and towns. I honestly did not have any idea at the time how long we would be gone, certainly not as long as we did. I realize now how selfish and thoughtless I was, and I was not aware Mai-Li demanded you leave. It was unfair and should not have happened.”

“I felt the same way at the time, however over the last couple of months, I reflected on Mai-Li’s position,” I stated. “She arrived at Blackfoot, inheriting hereditary status through her family lineage. Her main priority are the people of Blackfoot, and because of the dissention between me and Willie, she needed to deal with it. When I refused her compromise, she commanded me to leave. In my mind, taking Eddie from me was unforgivable, she knows how much he means to me, nonetheless she told me I was in no condition to care for a young boy on my own.”

Taylor started to speak, and I shook my head, I realized if I did not convey my distress and how I felt, I never would.

“I tried to visit with Eddie every day for over a week; yet she denied my appeal. On the day I left, she allowed me to talk with him. He was so brave and told me I had to heal, or in his words “get better.” It was then I understood, not only had I lost you I lost Eddie as well. I had no choice except to leave; there was nothing left for me in Blackfoot.”

Taylor shook his head, then took me in his arms. I stiffened; he did not free me. “Carlie, you have not lost me, you know how much I care about you, and I always will.”

I adamantly shook my head. "I am sorry Taylor; it is over between us. After we separated, and I had to leave, I did not know where to go or what to do. It was then, I realized how much I had come to rely on you."

"Do you have feelings for Lance?"

"I care about him; he was here when I needed someone in my life. I would not have survived on my own without him, one day my emotions will differ, and I will come to love him."

Taylor angrily released me, then turned and left. I composed my thoughts, then returned to the cabin. Lance and Pete were sitting at the table; Taylor was nowhere in sight.

The next couple of days were difficult, I kept to myself, I assisted in cooking the meals and keeping the cabin tidy. Taylor ignored me and refused to communicate; in the morning he disappeared for hours. The tension between Lance and Taylor was strained, and I spent time outside, absorbed in my artwork. Lance tried to communicate with me, and I did not respond, although I realized my reaction was not fair to him.

Days later, after eating supper, I retrieved *Peter Pan* from under my bedroll and turned to the page where I left off. Lance brewed a pot of tea, then joined Taylor and Pete at the table.

"Carlie," Pete requested. "Please join us."

I recognized his no-nonsense voice, marked my place in the book, and sat next to Lance. Pete took a sip of his tea, raised his head, and spoke.

"Carlie, there is a heaviness and sadness surrounding you; you carry an unbearable weight in your soul. The time has come for you to make choices in your life and move forward."

I took a deep breath and realized if I did not air my grievances, I would never find peace.

"You brought Willie to Blackfoot," I answered angrily, staring at Pete. "When you demanded I exonerate him, I rebutted, yet you allowed him to stay despite knowing how I felt and what I had endured."

Pete's face remained impassive.

"Mai-Li also insisted I pardon Willie. When I rejected, she banned me from Blackfoot and would not allow Eddie to come with me. To me, that was the most horrific retribution I've ever had to face."

I looked across the table at Taylor. "You knew Willie was with Pete from the onset and warned me if I refused to follow Pete's mandate, it would come between us, and I would lose you. Did you ever stop and reason how terrified I was facing Willie, how badly he hurt me? You were the sole person I felt would support me and losing you tore me apart."

Before he could rebut, I turned and faced Lance, realising I could lose his friendship forever when I shared my thoughts with him.

"Lance, without you I would not have survived these past months, you are a patient, considerate, and honourable man. I enjoyed the time we spent together, you taught me how to survive, how to appreciate the beauty of nature and how to have fun. You are a loyal companion, I care about you, however not in the way you want. I'm sorry."

Then I ran from the room. Lance rose to follow, and Pete called him back.

I sprinted to Taylor's wood shop and thought about the times he spent there with Eddie and Debbie. I recalled the laughter and screams when we took turns sliding down the hill on our makeshift toboggan. Christmas was magical, we decorated the tree, made gifts for each other, and Taylor pretended to be Santa Clause. I closed my eyes; I had no tears left to shed. I felt empty, and it was then I knew what I had to do.

I returned to the cabin and approached the table. The three men stopped speaking.

"I cannot return to Blackfoot and Princeton is not an option; I would not find work there as I have no training or skills. I will stay here at the cabin on my own."

Taylor and Lance started talking at the same time, and Pete raised his hand and intervened. "We must respect Carlie's wishes."

"Carlie, you can't do this, you're not prepared," Lance pleaded.

"In your mind, will I ever be? You have taught me so much, and I know inside if I do not change my past, it is as good as it's ever going to be for me."

Taylor rose, his face bitter. He turned and left the cabin, and I understood what we shared was finished.

"Carlie, I will respect your wishes. I will return to Blackfoot tomorrow with Grandfather and Taylor," Lance announced. "I'll take Ringo back with me, he is more than you can manage on your own, but I'll leave Thunder. If you need help in any way, turn Thunder loose and tell him to go home. If you decide to return, give him his lead and he'll come straight back to Blackfoot."

Before he left, Lance gave me instructions about Thunder's care. I must exercise him daily, even if it meant riding in circles around the corral; made sure his water trough was full and chat with him so he would not get lonely. I laughed at his instructions; when he raised his eyebrows and frowned, I realized he was serious.

The three men packed their supplies on their horses. Lance spoke to Pete, then he joined me on the porch. I felt uncomfortable when I looked at him, he smiled, then leaned over and kissed me.

"Don't discount what you have learned, do not lose yourself in your art, especially if you are away from the cabin. Stay alert."

I nodded, fighting back tears. "Lance, I so sorry..."

"Don't apologize, when the time comes, and you have chosen the right path, you will know who you want to be with."

"I hope we will always be friends, and if we are meant to be together, then it will happen."

Lance turned and looked towards the corral. Pete waited patiently for his grandson to join them. Taylor was on Lucy. He was watching us, his jaw rigid, his face flushed in anger.

"I know you don't want to admit it, even so, there is someone else who's in love with you and will fight to win you when the time comes," Lance murmured.

I said nothing; Taylor and I had not parted amicably, and I was angry and felt betrayed. "I must leave, we have a long ride ahead of us," Lance added. "We will not stop during the night; we will travel straight to Blackfoot."

He hugged me, then joined Taylor and Pete at the corral. As they rode away, Lance turned and waved, and I raised my hand in farewell. Taylor rode rigidly, ignoring me. When the four horses disappeared into the shadows, I went inside the cabin.

That night I did not sleep well and the next morning I woke disoriented and lost. My first task was to make a list of what I intended to do every day. By the time I got to page three, I realized how ludicrous my expectations were. My daily chores were to weed, water and compost the garden, clean the corral, and make sure I took care of Thunder. I didn't need a list to remember that.

I worked on my drawings and paintings and soon felt the overwhelming loneliness. I was also bored and needed more stimulation. I must broaden my search and uncover new areas to sketch. I recalled Lance's map he found in his grandfather's cabin, and when we arrived here, he placed it in the kitchen drawer, he never carried it on any of our excursions as he knew the area better than the back of his hand. It would not surprise me he left it behind on purpose.

The Tulameen River flowed east as well as west of the cabin, and as Lance and I had taken the western trail to the Tulameen Falls, I decided to try the eastern route. I packed a lunch and my canteen, my sketchbook, pencils and crayons, rifle, and ammunition. As Lance informed me previously, the terrain was rugged and heavily forested, if I ever decided to leave the main trail to explore on my own, he warned me to take a roll of red tape along as markings.

I saddled Thunder, tied on the pannier, and steered him towards the woods. At first, he refused to behave, and when I persisted, he gradually settled down. We passed an area of wild herbs and blueberry bushes, and I decided to mark the location. It was close to the cabin, and I would be thankful remembering where I found them when I foraged later in the year. I leaned over to tie the tape around one of the branches, when suddenly Thunder bolted. I tightened my hold on the reins, and from the corner of my eye, noticed movement in the grass and weeds bordering the path. I was excited when I glimpsed a rubber boa. They are elusive and rarely observed during the day as they were nocturnal. They were a gentle creature, non-aggressive and existed on mice and smaller rodents. I scolded Thunder and he picked up his pace as we passed the serpent. I made a mental note to keep in mind Thunder hated snakes.

I rode along the river and travelled a short distance, then caught sight of an overgrown trail. I turned onto it and had not ridden far when the path took a sharp turn to the left.

"Whoa" I called out, as I pulled on the reins. I was facing the aftermath of wildfire; a subject Lance was knowledgeable about and which we discussed often. He adamantly warned me, especially if I had no idea how old the wildfire might be, to never stray into the burned-out area due to the danger of fallen trees and hidden debris. Once grasses, flowers and fireweed started to grow, it was a sign of the beginning of ecosystem recovery, a part of the natural cycle of fire and regeneration.

I dismounted and tied Thunder to a cedar surrounded by an abundance of grass and wildflowers. I paced carefully around the edge of the scorched area and viewed the reshaped landscape, burned trees, and blackened stumps. I removed my supplies and sat on the edge of the path and spent the afternoon quick sketching the devastation and loss. I visualized the final work, the twisted tree stumps, and the magenta-pink flowers of the fireweed covering the ground.

I stopped and ate a quick lunch, and when my neck and back complained, I packed my gear and left. I arrived back at the cabin an hour later.

I made a quick supper; leftover pheasant and vegetables picked yesterday from the garden. Exhausted, I decided to go to bed early. I woke early the next morning, finished my chores, then spent the rest of the day painting. I paused to rest when a random notion struck me. Why not expand my research, I could show the damage inflicted on the landscape by wildfires, the occurrence of water contamination, and how nature responded by regeneration of new trees. Lance and I often discussed The First Nation's role; they believed fires were an ancient force of nature that shaped ecosystems. One of the first wildfires on record in Canada occurred in 2023. As time passed, they occurred more often, became more severe, and occurred earlier in the season. Climate change overturned conventional tactics to tree planting and fire management.

The residents of Blackfoot integrated their cultural insight into restoration strategies. They believed reshaping landscapes, adapting new tactics, building resilient forests, and creating fire-adapted communities were an integral part of recovery. It was much more than just transplanting trees, it was a process that needed long-term vision, science, and deeper engagement with Indigenous-led practices.

Discovering my passion to research wildfires lifted my spirits, I coveted to share my insight with Lance although I knew it was not possible. I looked at the map and was surprised to discover the trail I took that led to the wildfire was marked with a star. I spotted several more on the map, in various locations, and chuckled quietly. Lance was not physically present; however, I detected his spirit. Stumbling across his gift would cut my search time down drastically.

The next day, I ate quickly, packed the tent and provisions, mounted Thunder, and headed towards the closest location marked on Lance's map. It was located west of the cabin, and I steered Thunder down the same path we took when we went to the Tulameen Falls. It took almost two hours to reach the transformed landscape; the rugged and unyielding peaks of Treasure Mountain rose sharply in the background creating a stark contrast against the bare rock and burned meadow once littered with tiny ponds. I pictured myself portraying this view and was anxious to return to the cabin, I felt it would be one of my better images.

I installed the tent and started a campfire. I made a pot of coffee, poured some into my cup, and began to sketch, focusing on my task, I did not stir until I detected a movement behind me. I spun around, realizing how late it was. Thunder was standing behind me, munching on grass and shrubs. When we arrived, I tied him to a tree branch and lost track of time. I poured water into his dish and stroked his muzzle, hoping he would excuse my negligence.

I put my art equipment in the tent, grabbed my rifle, and returned to the campfire. I stirred the coals and reheated the coffee. The leftovers from yesterday's supper were tasty. Lance's advice to me about losing myself in my artwork and staying alert came to mind. Thank goodness Thunder couldn't share his thoughts, or I would be in deep trouble.

I retired early yet could not relax. Had I made the right decision, would I succeed, living on my own. It was necessary I let go of disagreeable memories and focus on moving forward.

Chapter Eighteen

My decision to research wildfires kept me active, and I sketched, painted, and wrote about the transformed landscapes, the regrowth of grasses, flowers, and aspen shoots. Often, I came across an older wildfire and was astonished by the abundant array of purple fireweed and morel mushrooms. Lance mentioned this phenomenon to me several times, and I made a point of writing about them. How I wished he were here with me; there was so much he could teach me.

The days grew warmer, and I watered the garden daily. The vegetables grew rapidly, and I often made a salad for a meal. I tried eating dandelions, except I found them bitter. Stinging nettles had a distinct flavour all their own and were abundant in late summer. At times, while out looking at new wildfire sites, I would trap a pheasant or grouse and pick nodding onions to add flavour to the stew. I searched for berries, hazelnuts, and edible roots, how I wished I watched Mai-Li closer when she cooked for our group on our journey to the Interior.

Time passed quickly, and I kept busy with my research and artwork. When it was sweltering outside, I would strip to my underwear and wade in the creek. After supper, I sat outside on the porch and recalled cherished memories and discussions I shared with Lance. The solitude at times was bittersweet, had I made the best decision to stay by myself at the cabin? If I did not absolve Willie, I would not be able to return to Blackfoot. The idea of going to Princeton frightened me, I knew a bit about protecting myself, however, not enough to survive on my own.

I missed Eddie more each day and realized he was safe and taken care of by Mai-Li and Taylor. His affection and patience for Debbie would help him mature into a kind, youthful man. One day Taylor would meet someone he cared for, someone who would escort him on his expeditions.

A week passed, and I decided to explore a new area. I woke early, packed my provisions, and headed south towards Podunk Creek, travelling on the Tulameen Forest Service Road. I stopped to make quick sketches of the creek, the scenery was remarkably like the area near the Tulameen Falls, and I decided to head back to the cabin. It was early afternoon, and I would be home in time to put some time into my painting before I retired at the end of the day.

Rather than ride back on the Service Road, I decided to check for an alternate route I could take. Lance's map showed there were two tributaries that flowed off the Podunk and headed northwest, both ending close to the cabin. I steered Thunder across the creek and arrived at the Hudson Bay Company Trail. The road was in rough shape, huge cedars and firs had fallen across it, making it difficult for Thunder to navigate around them. At one point, we passed the skeletal remains of a wildfire. I wrote the location and information down in my sketchbook as a later reference.

We soon arrived at Chisholm Creek, which bordered a narrow trail. I did not go far, when an acrid, pungent odour infiltrated the air. I stopped Thunder, dismounted, and edged into the bush. A thin haze of smoke wafted upward; I peered from behind a gigantic cedar and caught sight of a dishevelled older man sitting at a campfire. At first, I did not recognize him, then when I realized who it was, my stomach lurched as I recalled our last encounter. I inched my way back to Thunder, mounted and gently nudged him forward. The thick foliage and bush slowed his progress.

Branches snapped, and leaves rustled as heavy footsteps pounded behind us.

"Stop, or I'll shoot," a raspy voice shouted.

I spotted a thicket of trees to my left, and I steered Thunder towards them. When we arrived, I dismounted and led him deeper into the bush. He snorted and I touched his withers and whispered softly. He at once settled down. If I tried to return to the main trail, I would be an open target.

I poured water from my canteen into my hands and let Thunder drink. I took a tiny swallow, saving the rest. When he got fidgety, I calmed him, thankful for his common sense and training.

Since taking cover, I detected no movement; I hoped the unwelcome guest would return to his camp. I was not sure if he was alone, and assumed he was on foot, as I did not notice any horses at his campsite.

I climbed on Thunder's back and steered him back to the main trail. This morning, it had taken me almost two hours to arrive at Podunk Creek. I followed Chisholm Creek for half an hour, and if my calculations were correct, I was an hour and a half from the cabin. Thunder hated being followed, and if I were being tailgated, he would warn me immediately. I removed my rifle and pulled back the hammer, engaging the firing pin. I gripped it in my left hand and tightened my grip on the reins and urged Thunder to pick up speed.

I focused on the surroundings; something was off, it was too quiet. I brought Thunder to a standstill. I heard movement behind me, when suddenly my arm was seized, and I dropped my rifle. Then I was forcefully pulled from the saddle and landed heavily on the ground. I tried to escape from his iron grip, I screamed and kicked, struggling for my life.

"Stop fighting me," a hoarse voice ordered. "Shooting you and leaving you here in the woods to rot don't bother me none."

I stopped and looked up in disbelief.

"What in hell are you doing out here all by yourself?" an enraged voice roared.

I refused to answer, knowing full well it would not take much to provoke him.

"Ain't talking, fine with me. I was aware you were watching my camp; I knowed it was you right off. I left my belongings back there, so you and me is going on a hike."

Then he strolled towards Thunder, snatched the reins, and yanked them firmly. The startled horse snorted and turned sharply; he was never handled roughly, and I knew he would fight back.

The sound of a cocked rifle alerted me. "Don't you dare harm him, Lars," I yelled as I rolled towards my rifle. Regrettably, Lars was standing next to it, he kicked it to the side, then bent and picked it up, and pointed it at me. Then he motioned for me to stand.

"Figured that would grab your attention," he threatened. "I'd be dim witted if I did anything to that horse, he's my ticket out of here."

Lars pulled Thunder's reins back and tried to mount. The startled horse spun in a circle, pulled his head back and neighed in frustration. Lars yanked the reins sharply.

"Don't," I commanded. "He'll keep fighting you, then he'll run off and we'll both be on foot."

"No horse is goanna git the better of me. He'll soon know who's in charge."

"I doubt it, he's spirited, has a mind of his own, and extremely strong. You won't win."

Lars swore under his breath. "You're sure as hell aren't gitting on his back, I ain't that stupid."

"Fine, we'll hoof it to your camp and use him to carry the supplies."

"Soon as we git there, you can let me know where West is hiding."

I inhaled sharply, now it made sense, he was looking for information about Taylor, and once he received it, I would be of no further benefit to him. He would discard me, one way or the other.

"I haven't seen him in ages," I shrugged indifferently. "The rest of the group moved on."

"I ain't the least bit interested in your group of misfits," he spat. "It doesn't surprise me none about West though, he never cared 'bout nobody 'cept himself."

I had to steer Lars away from digging for information about Taylor.

"Are you out here on your own?" I inquired, staring directly at him. "What happened to the Desert Rats?"

His face reddened; had I overstepped my boundaries? Lars was mean tempered at the best of times; it would not take much to provoke him.

"Decided it was time to move on," he answered angrily. "Ain't nothing left 'cept howling winds and desert in the Wastelands."

I did not believe he left the Desert Rats by choice. His reputation was volatile, and it would not have surprised me if they barred him from the Wastelands.

It was clear Lars still held a grudge against Taylor, stemming back to Little Mountain when Taylor challenged and defeated him and took over leadership of the Phantoms. They clashed again when we had an altercation in the Wastelands with Lars' band, the Desert Rats. Lars swore he would recover the three rifles and ammunition Taylor had stolen. The bad blood between Lars and Taylor was not settled; and would not be until they confronted each other.

My loathing and revulsion towards Lars ran deep and would always remain with me, I blamed him for Rusty's death.

Lars glared at me, "You ain't carrying a lot, just enough for a coupla' days. You live close by?"

I experienced a sinking sensation in my stomach; the last thing I needed was Lars to find out about the cabin. If I tried to hightail it, I might be able to outrun him; but I refused to abandon Thunder. Lars would not hesitate to mistreat him if he could not control him. I did not have any choice except to divulge where I resided, and it would not take him long to realize I was on my own.

"I don't live far from here," I replied. "Returning to your campsite to retrieve your supplies would take approximately one hour, then another two hours to arrive at my place."

"I ain't got much choice, do I?" Lars snorted, as he spat on the ground. "Control your horse, and don't do anything stupid; you try running off, I'll shoot him, it sure ain't worth having a horse who ain't trained and can't be ridden."

Lars seized the reins and left. I sidled to Thunder's far side and stroked his neck. It was evident he disliked Lars, and I cannot say I blame him.

It did not take long to reach Lar's campsite. He put me to work packing his supplies. When he tried to remove my provisions from Thunder's back, I strongly rebutted. My sketching pad, art supplies, and notes, which did not take a lot of space, were irreplaceable.

"I won't leave anything behind," I snapped. "My provisions go where I go."

"Are you always this cantankerous?" he asked harshly.

"If I'm fighting for what's mine. Neither of us is riding, there's plenty of room."

We soon packed all the gear on Thunder's back, I led him towards the path, and Lars grabbed and twisted my arm.

"Don't try anything stupid, go straight to your place, and do what I say. I have your weapon, which looks a lot like the rifle your boyfriend stole from me."

I turned my back to him and picked up my pace. Under my breath I whispered quietly. "He's not my boyfriend anymore."

Chapter Nineteen

Thunder fought Lars all the way, adding to our travelling time. The sun dropped behind the horizon, darkness deepened, and moonlight streamed through the gnarled tree branches that snaked upward. Rustling leaves announced our presence, and an owl hooted, accompanied by a serenade of crickets.

Lars dug out his flashlight and turned it on. The power was low, and I hoped it would last until we reached the cabin. Wandering alone in total darkness with a madman was not something I relished.

Hours passed, and just when Lar's flashlight lost power we arrived at the cabin. There was enough moonlight to unload the supplies on the porch, which Lars forced me to do while he stood and watched. When I took Thunder to the corral, he stayed close behind us, it was obvious he did not trust me and was quite aware I would try to escape the first chance I got. It was light enough for me to remove Thunder's tack and pour water into his trough. Stalling for time, I found the curry comb and started grooming him; Lars seized it and tossed it over the fence and into the brush. Then he pushed me out of the corral and secured the gate.

Drained and lethargic, I climbed the steps to the porch and entered the cabin. "I can't see a thing in here," I muttered. "I'll light the lantern and then bring the supplies in."

Lars grunted and watched me closely as I trudged into the shed. I returned with the propane lantern, struck a match, and lit it. Then I hauled the supplies inside and put them in a corner.

"I'll unpack in the morning," I advised. "I have some chores to deal with first."

"That can wait until tomorrow," Lars sneered.

I ignored his outburst, took the water canister and the lantern, and moved towards the shed. When I tried to open the door, Lars stood in my path. "Move," I snapped angrily. "I need to go to the creek to fill the canister, unless you want to drink contaminated water, and I also want to check and make sure the garden's irrigation system is working. It if isn't, you won't be eating either."

Lars scowled, and at that moment I did not care if he was upset or not. He gestured towards the back door, and I stepped outside. He was directly behind me and if he persisted in guarding me so closely, there was no way I could make a run for it.

I stopped at the garden and inspected Lance's filtration system; it was working well and reminded me of him. How I wished he were here; his projection that Lars might be in the area was accurate, and I wouldn't be in this predicament either if I hadn't insisted on staying here on my own.

Lars lumbered awkwardly behind me as I sidled down the hill to the creek. I set the lantern on the ground and waded into the water and filled the canister. He did not offer to help me carry either of them back to the cabin and when I tripped over a rock, he shoved me aside. Cursing under my breath, I stumbled to keep from falling.

Huffing and puffing from his climb, Lars followed me into the shed, then into the main room of the cabin. I set the lantern on the table and placed the water jug on the floor next to the stove.

"It's too late to start the stove," I muttered. "I'll boil the water in the morning before it gets hot outside."

Lars did not respond, he looked around the cabin, then sauntered over to the larger mattress. I braced myself, ready to hightail it, I did not trust the man further than I could throw him.

"This place is in excellent shape, a garden, plenty of chopped wood, and food in the shed. Somebody put a lot of work into it. How come there's so many beds; you lie to me 'bout others living here?"

I hesitated to answer, should I pretend I was waiting for the return of the others, would Lars become cautious and decide to leave? Witnessing his hostility in the past reminded me how much he distrusted people, and if he decided to stay and discovered my deception, he would retaliate with cruelty. I had to produce a feasible story.

"Last year, after your group caught up to us and you agreed to return to the Wasteland," I answered guardedly, "We climbed around Mount Davis and headed north. It was pure luck finding this cabin, and realizing the weather could turn any day, we decided to spend the winter here. The place was empty and in horrible shape, so we cleaned it and Taylor fixed the stove. When spring arrived, we left and eventually arrived at Blackfoot."

"Still can't figure out why you're here alone; it was obvious West had the hots for you; I can't see him chucking you. What really happened?"

The man may be the most repulsive human being I'd ever met, but unfortunately, he was cleverer than he looked. I would be foolhardy to push him.

I did not, however, intend to disclose the reason I was here was because of Willie. The less he knew about that situation the more comfortable I would be.

"Every adult person in Blackfoot was supposed to contribute to the welfare of the town; since I had no vocation or training in any field, I was expected to leave. Princeton was out of the question; people are struggling there to survive.”

“You expect me to believe that bullshit,” he threatened heatedly.

It was obvious Lars was digging for information about Taylor. Although Taylor and I parted bitterly, I could not let Lars know where he was. If he found out, he would not hesitate to go after him.

“It didn’t take long for the residents to discover Taylor’s aptitude and skill with weapons. He joined a hunting party from the Similkameen band. I had no idea where they went, or how long he would be gone. Again, as I told you, I was by myself, I could not pay my way; that’s the reason I had to leave, and why I’m here.”

Lars looked up at me, then moved closer. Alarmed, I stepped back, prepared to run. He smirked; aware I was afraid of him.

“You’re still lying through your teeth, personally I don’t give a shit why you’re here on your own, or where the rest of your motley crew ended up. All I want is West. If you do what you’re told, I won’t bother you. If you try to take off, you won’t make it far, then I’ll get mean.”

The next few days were gruesome, I cooked, cleaned, chopped wood, weeded the garden, kept the water canister full, scrubbed the woodstove, and picked up after my unwanted guest. Lars ate most of the food, leaving me the scraps. He confiscated the larger mattress, and when he was awake, he was abusive and would threaten me if I did not move fast enough. He stopped short of physically abusing me as I did all the work, and he reaped the benefits. It was akin to living with a slovenly pig, obviously cleanliness was not part of his personal hygiene; I got into the habit of bathing in the creek with my clothes on.

Early one morning, when Lars was still asleep, I gathered my paint and brushes, sketchbooks, finished canvases, and my notes on wildfires, stuffed everything inside one of the bags I found in the shed, then tiptoed down to Taylor's wood shop and hid it under his work bench. I did not want to take the chance Lars found them, if he did, he would not hesitate to burn them in the stove. I had contributed substantial time researching and recording what I unearthed, hoping one day I could share my work and have it recognized and valued for its significance. If anything happened to me, someone would find where I had hidden them.

Days passed, it was late afternoon, and conditions had not improved. Lars got angrier and meaner, and I knew his mind was focused on Taylor. It did not take much for him to fly into a rage and I knew I was no match for his strength. I kept out of his way and watched him closely.

The weather remained brutally hot, and Lars spent most of the day sleeping. Food was in short supply and thankfully we had the garden and berry bushes close by. I asked Lars for permission to hunt for small game, but he refused to give me my rifle.

Lars continuously harassed me for Taylor's whereabouts, and I knew he was close to his breaking point. I had no intention of being around when he got physical. If I planned to escape now was the time.

I rushed to the corral and untied the gate. I lifted Thunder's saddle off the fence and reached for the reins hanging beside it. Suddenly, a thunderous roar resonated across the yard and Lars barrelled across the yard. I dropped the saddle, climbed on Thunder' back, and struggled to open the gate wider. Lars arrived just as Thunder went through the opening, he reached over the railing, gripped my arm tightly and yanked me off Thunder's back. I landed heavily on the ground. Remembering Lance's instructions to give Thunder free rein if I was ever in trouble I screamed. "Thunder, go home."

Lars raced towards the open gate, Thunder tore past him and bolted into the trees. Realizing what I had just done, Lars turned and faced me. "You bitch," he shouted, as he pulled me up. Then he slapped my face and hauled me back to the cabin and dragged me into the shed. He spotted a rope hanging on a nail, made me sit on the floor, then trussed my feet.

"Let's find out how long you can go without food and water," he threatened, as he slammed the door.

I lost track of time, not knowing how long I was tethered in the shed; I sensed Lars movement in the cabin, muttering angrily under his breath. The light under the door went out, and I was in total darkness. My mouth was parched, I suffered from dehydration, my jaw was tender from where he slapped me, and my body ached from lying on the wood floor.

I knew Thunder would sprint straight home, and with his speed and knowledge of the back trails, he would make it in record time. Lance would know at once something was amiss and would come to the cabin. If I could survive the next two days, I might come through this alive.

The old Carlie would have been placid, accepting what happened; not anymore. I carried my knife and as soon as it was safe, I would cut the rope and hightail it out of here. The darkness in the room was oppressive, I struggled to a sitting position, reached inside my boot, and gripped the hilt of my knife. I pulled it from its sheath, and holding it tightly, I began cutting the rope. I picked up movement in the cabin, then footsteps approaching the shed. I slid the knife back into the sheath, covered my boot with my jeans, then rolled over on my side. The door swung open, Lars stood in the doorway clutching the lantern. I pretended to be asleep, he muttered angrily under his breath, partially closed the door, shuffled back to the mattress, then snuffed out the light.

It was not long before his snores echoed through the cabin; I cautiously removed the knife and returned to cutting the rope. My arms and body ached, I realized I wasted valuable time, and I picked up my pace. The knife slipped, and I inhaled when I cut my ankle. I kept cutting until I felt the rope unravel, I unwound it, pulled it off and tossed it in a corner. I replaced my knife to my boot and waited. There was no sound coming from the cabin, and if I wanted to escape, I had to move now.

I stood and winced as my cramped muscles complained. I reached down and touched the cut; it was not deep and would soon clot.

I shuffled over to the wall and pressed my right hand against it for support. I headed towards the location of the back door, took a couple of steps, and touched the sleeve of my jacket. I had left it hanging on a peg, I reached up, removed it, and put it on. I then crept to the door, unfastened the latch, and opened it. It squeaked in protest, and I froze, my heart racing. I waited for the deafening roar from the cabin. I stepped outside and heard the rustle of leaves and a gentle wind stirring through the branches.

I sidled towards the outhouse, then shadowed the bush line, passed the corral, and headed down the trail. Running would be risky as the trees and foliage concealed the moonlight. It would be too easy to trip over a tree root or a protruding rock. I had to preserve my energy; I was hungry and exhausted from lack of sleep.

Then I recalled what Lance told me, if for any reason I sent Thunder to Blackfoot, the faithful horse knew the direct route to Blackfoot Road which turned into a trail that headed south to the Town of Blackfoot. He also knew the shortcuts Lance used when he rode through the dense woodlands enroute to Blakeburn. Would I be able to find his hoof prints on the path and detect if he had left the trail and taken the shorter route? It was too dark to see anything along the trail; I had to find cover and stay hidden until morning.

I looked behind me and spotted a moving light. Lars had discovered I had escaped! I made an immediate decision. I left the trail, turned left, and headed into the heavy bush. I spotted a huge cedar and scrunched under its low-lying branches. Hopefully, Lars would assume I was still in front of him on the path and would keep going, which allowed me time to head deeper into the forest and find shelter. I heard the wind in the branches, and the gentle rustle of leaves. An owl hooted in the distance, and animals scurried in the underbrush.

Taking flight would be dangerous, I had no idea which direction to take, and if I got lost in the heavy bush, I might not find my way out. I climbed the trunk of the cedar, moved onto a thick branch, and shimmied forward until I reached the node. I leaned back, then fell into a troubled slumber.

I woke with a jolt when the sun shone on my face. I stretched my legs, disoriented and sore from lying in an awkward position. Cedars, Douglas firs, pines, aspens, and alders surrounded me. It was vital I keep moving, Lars was an expert tracker, it would not take him long to realize I was no longer in front of him.

I clambered down the massive tree and thanked it for providing me with shelter, then turned northeast towards Blackfoot. With only a couple of hours of interrupted sleep and having no food or water in almost fifteen hours since Lars threw me in the shed, my energy was low.

I spotted a raspberry bush, gorged on the berries, and ate until my stomach protested. I picked up my pace. I had not gone far when I heard heavy footsteps behind me. I dashed behind an enormous lodgepole pine and was not surprised to see Lars standing next to a birch. Any sound or movement I made would give away my location. I took a deep breath, remained motionless, and prayed he would keep moving.

"I know you're close, you might as well show yourself."

I gritted my teeth; there was no way in hell I was going to reveal my location to him.

I inspected the area around me; to my right I spotted a raised embankment, long since taken over by erosion and sediment. It was steep and might provide a chance for me to hide and find cover. I inched over to the slope and lowered my foot over the ledge when suddenly the loam started to move, I scrambled to keep upright, lost my balance, and careened headfirst down the hill. I screamed, and the last thing I recalled was striking my head on a rock.

I slowly opened my eyes, overcome with nausea and dizziness, and felt a huge lump on my head. I spotted movement overhead and caught sight of Lars as he leaned over the ledge. I had fallen into a ravine and landed next to a bramble bush covered in thorny stems and leave. It was growing flush against the back wall of the ravine and unseen by Lars. I rolled on my stomach, gritted my teeth when a sharp muscle spasm hit my back. I edged gently under the shrub.

Lars marched back and forth on the rim of the slope, he kicked the ground angrily, then spat in disgust when he realized how steep the hill was, clearly aware he was in no shape to climb down and make his way back up. I lay motionless, breathing lightly. Lars did not have a lot of patience, which might work to my advantage.

"You down there, girly?" he yelled. When he got no response, he cursed loudly, then grabbed a handful of rocks and threw them over the ledge. Although he could not see me, he was aware I was at the bottom of the trench. I covered the back of my head with my hands, the projectiles landed in the middle of the ditch, and one hit the back of my leg. I clenched my teeth to stop from screaming. If I moved or made any sound, he would know I was still alive.

When Lars discovered I escaped from the shed, his first reaction would have been to grab his firearm. He was also carrying the propane lantern, and in his arrogance had miscalculated how far he would have to track me and had not brought his water flask. Lars was obese and suffered from the oppressive heat. He cursed loudly, then disappeared from my vision. His only alternative would be to backtrack to the cabin, and I knew him well enough to realize the only reason he left was because he assumed I was either dead or seriously injured and unable to climb back up the embankment.

The blazing sun shone relentlessly in the cloudless sky. There was no wind or relief. It was a waiting game; I was exhausted and weak from lack of food and water. I carried no weapons; I was in no shape to climb the bank and dared not take a chance I might fall. There had to be an alternate route. I had marched for over an hour before I took refuge in the cedar tree last night, then this morning, another hour before I arrived at the slope. Not knowing the extent of my injuries or how far I would be able to travel, I decided I had no alternative except to return to the cabin. I would hide in the surrounding undergrowth until dark, then take cover in Taylor's wood shop, which I doubted Lars knew existed.

Mentally, I calculated it was almost nineteen hours since I freed Thunder and Lars imprisoned me in the shed. Assuming Thunder took the hidden route, he should have arrived in Blackfoot by now and gone straight to Lance, who would know I was in trouble and would come as soon as he was able.

By now, Lars would have come to the same conclusion, he had two choices, he could remain at the cabin and take a chance no-one would come to my assistance, or he could pack up and go. He was lazy, manipulative, and cruel, which traits he exercised to coerce and dominate people. It would not surprise me if he chose to remain at the cabin, although, I hoped his search for Taylor would not compel him to leave and search for him; challenging Taylor would be the biggest mistake Lars would make in his life.

Chapter Twenty

The raised bank shadowed an old water source, long since dried up; the bottom of the trench, covered with cracked earth and dead, broken trees, looked hazardous and uninviting.

I pulled myself into a sitting position and listened for movement. I did not trust Lars; he could pretend to be gone and hide in the foliage next to the path and wait for me to show up. I leaned against the embankment and rested. I was partially out of the sun; and knew I could not stay hidden any longer, the sun would only become hotter, and I had no drinking water. I struggled to stand. The channel ran in two directions, and I did not know which way to turn. I squinted my eyes, looked up, and located where I placed my foot in the dirt that triggered my fall. The outline of my boot faced west, which was the direction where the cabin was located.

It was time to leave.

My progress was sluggish. I was dehydrated from the intense rays of the sun, my head pounded, and my heart raced. I removed my jacket and tied it around my waist. If I did not find shade soon, sun stroke would be the least of my worries.

I lost track of time and placed one foot in front of the other; I turned a corner and stopped. I shook my head in disbelief. The conduit had narrowed into a trail and disappeared. I faced a clearing surrounded by massive trees and heavy underbrush, and there was a noticeable difference in temperature. It was then I noticed a yew shrub and remembered its many attributes. Mai-Li, as well as Lance, were aware of its values and uses. I reached inside my boot and retrieved my knife, then cut off a branch. With what little strength I had left, I whittled it into a makeshift crutch.

I pushed myself remorselessly and checked for late berries, and passed a few bushes, stripped bare by the birds and animals. I had no inkling of my location; I discovered a route travelled by animals and followed it, hoping it would lead me the main trail.

I shuffled down the path and tripped over a tree root. I grabbed an overhanging branch and forced myself to keep walking. I lost track of time. I wanted to stop and rest; and knew if I did, I would not be able to get up again. I lurched around a bend and froze. I was facing the main trail.

Should I take cover in the trees and wait until dark? My energy was almost depleted and standing in the middle of the path deciding whether I should keep going or stay hidden was getting me nowhere. I staggered around a curve and froze; I shook my head in wonderment; I was facing the cabin. There was a light on inside, and I assumed Lars had returned. The corral was empty, had Thunder made it back to Blackfoot safely? Would help arrive soon?

The first thing to do was to find something to eat. I headed to the back of the lot and travelled along the side of the stream, wishing the water were drinkable. I recalled a conversation Lance and I had once regarding heat stroke and how dangerous it was to jump into a lake or stream to cool down. The best solution was to get out of the sun and find a cooler location.

I arrived at the vegetable garden and picked a ripe tomato. I lurched up the hill and entered Taylor's wood shop. I took a bite, my throat was dry, and I choked when I swallowed. Except the berries I found yesterday, it was the only food I had eaten in nineteen hours. I finished eating the tomato and wished I had the energy to go back to the garden for one more.

I lay my jacket on the ground and fell into a restless slumber. I jerked awake. It was sweltering and stuffy in the shop; I shivered and felt my forehead. I had a fever, and my body ached from the injuries I sustained from my fall. I crept outside, there was no movement near or inside the cabin. I staggered towards the creek, removed my shirt, and dunked it in the cool water. I swabbed it on my forehead, which provided some relief.

I put on my jacket and lay on the ground. Almost immediately my thoughts turned to Taylor. I recalled the hardships, perils, and adventures we shared. I missed his intimacy, his arms around me, his bittersweet kisses, and confessions of affection. The last time we spoke, we exchanged harsh words. I wiped the tears from my face and closed my eyes.

I awakened to the sound of galloping horses. I crept outside and glanced towards the cabin. The hazy, diffused light from the sunrise gave a soft edge to the landscaping. I sensed a man's outline in the shadows; I stumbled up the hill, when I reached him, he turned and I remember falling and being lifted in his arms.

I woke in the cabin lying on Taylor's mattress; his sleeping bag draped around me. Voices resonated cross the room. I raised my head and inhaled sharply. Willie was sitting at the table across from Taylor and when he noticed I was awake, he spoke quietly to Taylor, who lifted his head then joined me on the mattress.

I stared at Willie, then turned and faced Taylor. "Why is he here?"

Willie rose to leave, and Taylor glanced at him and shook his head.

"He's with me, Carlie," Taylor answered. "I know you anticipated Lance's return; however, he left on a spirit quest. When

Thunder arrived in Blackfoot, we realized something was wrong. I was prepared to come alone, and Pete suggested Willie join me, in case there was trouble.”

I found it awkward to look at Taylor and lowered my head.

“It was lucky Willie was with me; we ran into Lars on the trail. He took one look at us and tried to hightail it into the bush. I yelled for him to stop. He turned his rifle on me, and if Willie hadn’t fired a warning shot, Lar’s would not have hesitated to shoot.”

“He was carrying a couple of backpacks and two rifles,” Willie added. “After a closer look, we realized one of the packs and one of the rifles was yours. When we asked him where he got them, he fabricated a story about finding them at a vacant campsite.”

“It was clear he was lying and after some persuasion, he admitted they belonged to you.” Taylor added. “I demanded he tell me where you were and warned him, I would not tolerate any more lies. He shifted his story and admitted you disappeared, and he did not know where you were.”

“Then he clammed up, it was obvious he knew more than he let on,” Willie exclaimed.

I started to cough and struggled to catch my breath as a sharp spasm shot up my back. “Can I have some water?” I requested in a hoarse voice.

Willie poured water into a mug and brought it to me. I felt uncomfortable around him, and kept my head down as I drank, then I handed the cup to Taylor.

"Can I have some more?"

Taylor shook his head. "You need to drink slowly; you can have more later."

I lay back on the mattress and closed my eyes.

"Carlie," Taylor asked. "How did Lars end up with your backpack and rifle, and why do you look like a walking corpse."

"I don't want to discuss it."

"I do."

I knew Taylor would not stop coercing me until I told him what he wanted to know.

"A while back," I sighed. "I was out looking for landscapes to sketch when I came across his campsite. I knew it was him right away, and I tried to hide in the bush, I would be an open target on the trail. He tracked me and caught me, then took my gun. He tried to mount Thunder, but Thunder wouldn't let him near, I don't think he liked Lars very much."

"Smart horse," Willie muttered from across the room.

"Carlie, how did he find the cabin?"

"He threatened to kill Thunder if I did not show him where I lived, you know what he is capable of doing."

"It was the only thing you could have done." Taylor admitted.

"After that my life became a living hell, he forced me to wait on him. He made me do all the work, and I only got leftovers to eat.

He wanted information about you, and I told him we were no longer together, and I did not know where you were. He still blames you for taking over the Phantoms and stealing weapons at the Wastelands."

Taylor shook his head in exasperation. "Carlie, I am so sorry you went through hell with that bastard, although he won't show up again. We had a long, intense conversation and I warned him to leave the area at once and if he ever showed his face here again, he would have me to contend with."

"He'll probably head north to Princeton, there's no chance he will return to the Wastelands," I revealed. "When I grilled him as to why he left, he exclaimed there was nothing there but sand and firestorms. He didn't mention the Desert Rats, so I assumed they forced him to leave."

I rolled on my side and stared at the wall. My face and body ached; I was exhausted, hungry, and thirsty.

"I don't want to discuss Lars anymore," I moaned, finding it uncomfortable to breathe.

"Carlie, what's wrong?"

"I don't feel well."

"What happened?"

"It was evident things would soon get out of hand; Lars was about to lose control. He was losing patience with me since I would not disclose where you were. I waited until he dozed off, then I ran to the corral. I found Thunder's equipment; but I wasn't quick enough. Lars discovered I had escaped and saw me in the corral and before he could lock the gate, I released Thunder and told him to go home. Lars was furious, he hit me, then he tied me up in the shed, and told me I wouldn't receive any food or water."

Willie rose abruptly and slammed the door as he left the cabin.

"What's bothering Willie?" I spoke.

"He's okay," Taylor confessed. "Before we came here, we discussed what happened between the two of you. I imagine what you've just shared about Lars stirred up unwanted memories. It's something Willie must come to terms with, and you should know one of the reasons he came with me was to request your forgiveness."

I felt as if I was drowning, I pulled Taylor's bedroll over my head. "I can't, I can't," I cried.

"Carlie, that choice is yours, and only when and if you feel the time is right."

I lowered the bag and leaned against Taylor. "I'm glad you came instead of Lance," I whispered.

"Good to know," Taylor whispered.

I inhaled sharply and fought back tears.

Willie entered the room. He moved to the table and sat down. "Is it okay if I stay, Carlie?"

I nodded. Taylor turned and looked at me. "What happened after you escaped from Lars?"

"I'll share more when I feel better. I knew someone would know I was in trouble when Thunder arrived alone in Blackfoot. I was injured and in no condition to travel any distance; so, I decided to return to the cabin. I was not sure where Lars was, and I could not take a chance he was inside. That's why I hid in your wood shop."

"We are sorry Lance did not receive your message; he's on a spirit quest, being prepared to assume Pete's responsibilities as chief. As soon as he finds out you sent Thunder home, I am sure he'll show up."

"Once he discovers you and Willie are here, he'll know I'm safe."

Willie left the table and wandered to the shed. "I imagine you're hungry Carlie," he called. "Is it okay if I cook the grouse and veggies for supper?"

I turned and faced Taylor, my mouth opened in amazement.

"Sounds like a plan," Taylor answered.

"Willie...Willie's cooking?" I sputtered.

"He's an incredible cook," Taylor affirmed. "He's thinking about opening a restaurant."

"I guess that makes sense, he loves food, especially cookies."

"I can *HEAR* you," a voice called from the shed.

Taylor and I laughed, then Willie entered the cabin carrying a loaf with a lit candle in the middle.

"Happy 19th birthday Carlie," Taylor and Willie announced in chorus.

It was then I remembered what day it was. I blew out the candle.

"I don't reckon she likes it," Willie exclaimed in a twangy voice, "After all the work I done did making it and cooking it on top of this rusty, old stove."

"And don't forget all the time I spent trying to find that stupid candle," Taylor added.

I looked at Willie, "You poor dear. I imagine all you had to do was remove it from your fridge and wrap it up before you left Blackfoot."

Taylor laughed. "See Willie, you didn't fool her, she's way ahead of you."

Then I turned and faced Taylor. "And as for you, the candles were stored here in the cupboard next to the sink, you put them there yourself. Not really that tough to find."

Willie snickered and took the loaf over to the table to cut it.

"Is it chocolate?" I asked.

"Unfortunately, chocolate's hard to find in Blackfoot," Willie added. "You okay with ginger?"

"I love ginger, almost as much as chocolate."

Taylor was watching me, a wide grin on his face.

"You're such a jerk," I whispered.

Chapter Twenty-one

With Taylor's care, I gradually improved. He was not aware of the extent of my injuries until he assessed me. Willie took over the cooking and housekeeping chores, and I gawked at him in astonishment. I recalled when he joined our group at the warehouse at Little Mountain, and not once did he lift a hand. I suppose it takes some people longer to grow up.

Taylor was patient when I told him what I experienced after I escaped from Lars and fell into the ravine, finding my way back to the cabin, terrified Lars was behind me and what he would do to me once he caught me. Willie puttered around the cabin and took note of my story, but at times he left and disappeared. Taylor never mentioned it, and I was not prepared to discuss it.

Taylor insisted I keep moving, I wandered around the cabin, and ate whatever Willie cooked. Days later; Taylor decided it was time to change the scenery. He helped me dress in my shirt and jeans and made me sit on the porch steps while he chopped wood and replenished the pile in the shed. I enjoyed the comforting rays of the sun and the serene breeze as it ruffled my hair.

When he finished with the wood, Taylor joined me on the porch, carrying two mugs of water. He handed one to me.

"I'm going to clean the corral and groom the horses," he advised, as he gulped the water, then wiped his chin. "You okay sitting on the porch until I'm done?" he enquired as he handed me his empty cup.

I nodded and glanced at him as he strolled to the corral. It was then I realized there were four horses, not three. I assumed it was a supply horse, as it was evident I would not be doing any riding until I got better.

I sensed movement behind me; Willie was standing by the door.

"Hi Carlie. I was wondering if we could talk."

I stared up at him and nodded towards the steps. He sat down, and at first, I was uncomfortable being alone with him, then I realized before there could be any kind of development, we would have to communicate.

He stared at his hands, and I waited for him to begin. This would not be easy for either of us.

"I know how wrong I was, and I know how much I hurt you," he spoke. "I have no excuse regarding my actions, and I apologize."

I inhaled deeply and took a deep breath.

Willie wrung his hands, then continued. "It took me a while to grasp the impact of my actions, and I do not expect immediate forgiveness. I understand you require time and space to consider my request."

I remained silent, and I noticed Taylor watching from the corral. Suddenly a thought crossed my mind. "Did you talk to Taylor about this?"

Willie raised his head and nodded. "I mentioned it to him and asked what I should do."

I experienced immediate resentment and anger that he had discussed the matter with Taylor. Noticing my reaction, Willie said. "He said it was between you and me, and the only way anything could be resolved was for us to communicate with each other."

"I can hear Taylor saying that." I replied.

Willie lowered his head and waited. I realized I must be honest and direct if I expected any type of closure.

"I appreciate how difficult it is discussing this matter," I began. "It's a lot to take in, I have to consider it; when I'm confident you're remorseful and willing to change, I will let you have my answer."

"Thank you for being open-minded and fair with me, Carlie, and for now, I can't expect anything more." Willie answered solemnly. Then he turned and went inside the cabin.

The atmosphere around the cabin improved, and I was more relaxed around

Willie. At times, I found it awkward to communicate and talk candidly and appreciated he did not push me for an immediate absolution.

When I was able to walk longer distances, Taylor and I strolled down to the creek. We held hands, and when he kissed me, I tensed. Taylor pointed towards a patch of grass beneath a gigantic fir. We sat down and I waited patiently, aware he would talk when he was ready.

"Carlie, is something bothering you? When I approach you, I sense your hesitation. I know you're annoyed with me, only I'm not sure why?"

I struggled to stand; Taylor held my arm, and I turned angrily and pulled back.

"Don't," I ordered. "I don't want to discuss it."

"That's the way you always manage problems, isn't it; it's so much easier to bury it inside."

"Sometimes communicating doesn't work, I've learned that the harsh way."

"That may be true at times; but I've always been honest with you."

"Not all the time."

Taylor leaned away from me in disbelief, then ran his fingers through his hair. "I have always treated you with respect, when have I ever disrespected you?"

"When you asked me to marry you, you were aware that Pete had brought Willie to Blackfoot and vindicated him. You also insisted that I meet with Willie, warning that if I refused, it would create a rift between us. You knew how upset I was, and how I felt. When you left with Pete, I had no idea you had gone with him, or when you would return. Mai-Li demanded I absolve Willie as well, which I could not do, and then she banned me from Blackfoot. I asked her if you and Eddie would be going with me, and she told me you left days before with Pete and she presumed I knew. That's how I found out you had left me."

Taylor shook his head in denial, and I knew I had to keep talking, or this matter between us would never be resolved.

"Then she told me I was in no condition to care for a young boy on my own, and Eddie would remain with her. Parting from him was the most heart wrenching thing I ever had to do."

"Carlie, I am sorry, I told Mai-Li I was leaving with Pete; it was a last-minute decision, and I asked her to let you know. I did not realize my message had not been passed on to you."

"My life turned upside down that day, I lost you and I lost Eddie. I vowed I would do everything in my power to return and get him."

"When the time is right, we will go to Blackfoot and get Eddie."

"So, all I have to do," I replied, "is pardon Willie, even if I am not prepared to do so."

"You've taken the first step with him, and I know the two of you will never be close friends, but it's a beginning."

Taylor pulled me into his arms, and I turned and faced the creek.

"It's Lance you're brooding about; you're in love with him?"

I was not surprised with Taylor's question, and I understood what I told him now would decide the outcome of our future.

"When I first met him, he told me he was Pete's grandson and sent to escort me to my destination. I questioned Lance as to how Pete knew I would have to leave Blackfoot; he said he discussed the matter with Mai-Li and was aware she would ban me if I refused to condone Willie."

Taylor hesitated, inhaled deeply, and remained silent.

"We took a shortcut to the cabin. Thunder bucked me off, and I hurt my back, so Lance took me to Pete's place until I got better. Pete has a bathtub in his bedroom, and Lance heated water, and I took a bath. It really relieved the pain in my back."

Taylor frowned, averting my eyes. "A few days later, we continued our journey to the cabin. It didn't take Lance long to realize I had no idea how to survive on my own. He offered to stay, and I told him he must have duties to deal with in Blackfoot. He said he was worried about Lars and didn't want me to stay here on my own."

Taylor frowned. "How did Lance know about Lars?"

"I told him about your history with him, and our altercation in the Wastelands. For some reason that information remained with him. I'm grateful he decided to stay, he taught me about nature, survival, and the beliefs of the Similkameen people, and about climate change, and wildfires."

Taylor was rigid, I had no idea what he was feeling or thinking at the time.

"He brought me paint supplies, sketching pads and paper," I advised. "He knew I was interested in drawing, he remembered I took lessons from the artisans when I resided in Blackfoot."

"You definitely have a talent in that area," Taylor commented. "It was unfortunate your training discontinued when the problem regarding Willie developed."

"Things shift, Taylor. Hopefully one day I will find where I really belong, and with whom."

Taylor remained silent and waited for me to continue. "Lance took me to abandoned cabins, and to rivers, creeks and waterfalls, which I sketched, and painted."

I turned and faced Taylor, then added. "If Lance had left, I would not have survived. I owe him so much."

"Enough to fall in love with him."

"I thought I had, however when I saw you again, I knew it wasn't how I felt. He will forever be a close friend, and I learned so much from him. It wasn't until he left and returned to Blackfoot with you and Pete, I realized everything he taught encouraged me to expand my perspective. It was then I decided to develop my research and write about wildfires."

"Was that what you were doing when you ran into Lars?" Taylor questioned abruptly.

I nodded, wishing he would change the topic.

"Both Lance and I were aware Lars posed a threat," Taylor said. "There was no indication he was in the vicinity. Regardless, we should not have left you on your own."

"None of us knew he was in the area" I solemnly reminded him. "There's no way of knowing when an unforeseen event will occur, we were caught off guard."

Taylor shook his head in denial. "We argued when I pressured you about Willie, and instead of supporting you, I agreed to accompany Pete on his trip, not knowing where we were going or how long we would be gone. It was an opportunity to commence working on my research and I selfishly pushed aside your wellbeing. You faced Mai-Li on your own, which triggered your separation from Eddie, and then banishment from Blackfoot. If I were there, I would not have allowed it to happen."

"What would you have done Taylor, you know Mai-Li's commands cannot be ignored."

"Yet she has been sincere with all of us, including Willie, and would have listened. If we had not agreed on a compromise, then you, I and Eddie would have left Blackfoot."

"I had no idea you felt that way."

"Actions are just as powerful as words, Carlie, and it is time to make some crucial decisions. It took something like this to realize I never stopped loving you; although you still have a penchant of getting into trouble."

"I love you too, and I don't get into trouble."

"Hmm, the verdict is still out on that."

I stuck out my tongue and punched Taylor's arm.

"Ouch," he whispered, then he took me in his arms and kissed me.

Chapter Twenty-two

We soon had a routine; Taylor chopped wood, kept the corral clean and the horses fed; Willie weeded and watered the garden and cooked the meals, and I kept the cabin tidy and did the laundry.

A few days later, after sweeping the floor in the shed, I checked the food supply and discovered we were low on meat and herbs. I mentioned it to Taylor and Willie that night and suggested they go hunting the next day and with any luck, they might bag a deer or a moose. To make it more enticing, I told them to take the extra horse to carry their supplies and equipment.

It did not take too much convincing; they both went to bed early. It was dark in the cabin the next morning when they woke, eager to go. They packed and fed the horses and had them equipped and saddled before sunrise.

Taylor handed me my rifle and told me to put it somewhere close. "It's loaded; in case you receive unexpected company." I grimaced and took the weapon, and he noticed my reaction. "I hope you haven't forgotten everything I taught you on our travels?"

"No, I haven't, I just don't care for guns, that's all."

He crossed his arms, a warning he was in no mood to argue. "I know you don't, but it's important, it won't be long before you're living on your own."

Taylor retrieved his bow and arrows from the shed, then he and Willie headed towards the corral. I heated a bucket of water and enjoyed a much-needed sponge bath. I decided to read awhile and after searching, found *Peter Pan* tucked under my bedroll. I was halfway through chapter three when I dozed off. Even classics are boring when you've read them so many times you've memorized all the words.

I woke hours later and strolled outside and stood on the porch. The empty corral, the absence of voices and movement, left an impression of abandonment and emptiness. On our trek to the Interior and living at the cabin, Taylor and Willie hunted often and knew the topography well.

I sighed and went back inside. I puttered around the cabin, looking for imaginary dust. I wandered down to the garden and ate a handful of sweet peas and peelings. I went down to the stream and leaned against a cedar and watched a Stellar jay fly between the hanging branches of a Douglas fir.

How was I going to keep myself occupied when the guys returned to Blackfoot and I was living here on my own. I had received the choice to live with settlers or move to Princeton, yet I dismissed both opportunities.

What was I looking for? I knew I must find myself a project, something to keep me occupied in the months ahead. It was then I remembered my art supplies hidden in Taylor's wood shop. I raced down the hill and found the bag, then hauled it back to the cabin.

I chose one of my older sketches, took a sheet of canvass and started painting. Without warning, Taylor stepped up behind me, bent over, and kissed my neck. I yelped, dropped my brush, and fell backwards off the seat. He snatched me before I landed on the floor.

"Taylor, look what you made me do?" I scolded irritably. "I dropped my brush, now I have to do this part all over again."

Taylor leaned over and studied my artwork. "Carlie, this is great. Where is this place?"

"It's Tulameen Falls. Lance took me, I drew sketches and quick outlines, and then I would paint them when I got back to the cabin. I told you about it earlier."

"Is that a pool under the falls?"

"Uh hu, Lance and I swam in it, we raced, and I almost beat him."

"I didn't know you owned a bathing suit."

"I don't."

Taylor looked at me, his eyebrows raised.

"I wore my jeans and shirt," I quickly added.

"And Lance?"

"He wore mumble...mumble......mumble.........

"I didn't catch that, what did you say?"

"Look Taylor, this is where the water flows into the pool and forms a mist, you can take a shower in there if you want."

"A shower?"

I glanced at Taylor, his eyes narrowed, then his face turned a deep red. Before I could ask what was wrong, a burst of laughter erupted from the far side of the room. Willie was leaning against the wall, clutching his stomach.

"You think that's funny?" Taylor sputtered, walking towards him.

"Totally man." Willie answered.

I gripped Taylor's hand and got his attention; then decided it was time to change the topic. "I assume your hunt was successful."

Taylor and Willie started talking at the same time, and I heard their extended tale on how they rode for hours, found a bull moose, tracked it into unknown territory, and finally bagged it. They carved and wrapped it in the tarp and returned to the cabin. Both thanked me in suggesting they take the extra horse.

"Tomorrow we'll start a fire and smoke the meat," Taylor suggested. "You still have your grill and smoker, Carlie?"

"It's somewhere in the shed; I'll find it later. Does that mean we're having roast for supper tomorrow?" I said, looking at Willie.

"I'm contemplating it?"

I shook my head. "Super, as long as you cook it, I'll eat it," I responded.

Willie chuckled, and Taylor shook his head. If he still had plans for our future together, I saw no reason he shouldn't discover what to expect from me regarding my lack of cooking skills.

The days passed quickly, there was always something to keep us busy.

Late one afternoon, Taylor and I were standing next to the garden, and he mentioned how impressed he was with the irrigation system and the variety vegetables. I told him Lance's mother gave him a bag of seeds when he returned to Blackfoot for supplies and food while I waited at the lean-to, then Lance designed and installed the irrigation system.

Taylor nodded, and we watched a graceful butterfly flutter among the peas.

"It's almost time to pick and preserve the last of the vegetables," I mentioned.

Taylor scratched the back of his head, then turned and faced me. "Carlie, it won't be long before the weather changes and winter arrives; it's necessary we make some positive plans."

I had anticipated this moment; it was time to let him go.

I took a deep breath and murmured. "I know, and I'm so grateful you and Willie stayed as long as you did; when do you mean to leave?"

"Willie will be returning tomorrow, I'm not sure if you know; he's searching for his mother, you might recall when we were hiking to the Interior, he told us she left him and his dad when he was only ten."

"Yes, I do. I find it difficult to believe he is doing that, although he has matured over the past year, and it makes sense. Has he achieved any success?"

"That is why it is necessary he return, just before Thunder arrived in Blackfoot, Willie discovered his mother's whereabouts and decided to go to Princeton to find her, which ironically is where he found her. She finds work when she can, sadly she struggles with poor health and is barely surviving. As Lance was unavailable to come here, Willie put his trip on hold and offered to accompany me. We mentioned the possibility the two of you might have an altercation, but as we had no idea how serious your situation was, we decided it would be wiser that both of us provide support rather just one of us. Willie is gradually coming to terms with his past discrepancies and is trying to make amends."

I nodded in agreement. "When he talked to me about pardoning him, I wasn't sure if he was sincere. We came to a mutual decision, and I told him I would when I was ready."

"It's a beginning, Carlie, you'll know when the time comes."

"You told me Willie would be leaving tomorrow, aren't you going with him?"

"I've requested he pass on a message to Pete. If you are agreeable, I will stay here, I know you are trying to come to terms about where you and I stand. Spending time together might aid both of us in coming to a resolution. We will never find happiness if we cannot find peace."

I nodded in agreement, praying I made the right decision. Could we make it work?

The next morning, Willie packed his supplies and mounted Gus. Taylor leaned over and placed his hand on Willie's knee. "Do us a favour, would you check on Eddie and tell him we are both okay, and we miss him very much, and as soon as we can, will come back for him. We have no intention of spending the winter here; Carlie and I want to sort out a few glitches before we return."

Willie nodded and steered Gus towards the path. We watched as they disappeared around the bend.

"I told Willie to talk to Pete or Mai-Li about bringing his mother to Blackfoot, she will be welcomed," Taylor told me as we strolled back to the cabin.

"Perhaps he'll find some closure," I murmured.

That evening after supper, Taylor and I chatted for hours. I told him it did not take Lance long to realize how inexperienced I was living on my own and decided to stay with me at the cabin. We explored deserted towns, isolated landscapes, and eventually I discovered the destruction, and beauty of the aftermath of wildfires, and began sketching and writing about them.

I showed Taylor my drawings and he was impressed and believed I had uncovered an area I could explore and would be of interest to many people.

Occasionally, our conversations were about Taylor and his travels with Pete; one of the topics addressed was the reclamation of the vacated towns and mines. Over the years, there was ongoing research conducted by the residents of Blackfoot, and eventually it was agreed to rebuild and repopulate them. With so many metropolitans and enormous cities destroyed by earthquakes and wildfires, people struggled to survive and given an opportunity, would have the choice to move to the rebuilt towns and start a new life. They would be encouraged to cultivate gardens, set up fruit orchards, and raise poultry, goats or livestock such as pigs or cows. The concept of living off the land was encouraged.

Taylor mentioned he had documented material regarding the deserted mining towns they visited, the deterioration and damage suffered over the years and if it would be possible to rebuild. Some of the villages and mines were devastated by fire or natural disasters, making reconstruction impossible.

"Your artistic talent would have been invaluable; it would have recorded my research."

"Lance and I roamed through the old towns, and I made sketches, and captured them on canvas when we got back to the cabin. You're welcome to look at them if you care to."

"I would enjoy that so much, Carlie. With cameras, videos, and iPads no longer available, handwritten records will eventually become priceless."

I hung on to Taylor's words as he discussed what he experienced and identified his passion about renewal and rebuilding. I experienced similar emotions about the land and forests destroyed by wildfires.

"I am genuinely interested in wildfires, particularly by the damage inflicted by them." I told Taylor. "I found their locations on Lance's map, and wrote about them, and sketched them, especially those that appealed to me. Is that something we can study and research?"

"Carlie, I don't know why we can't merge my work and your research."

"I would love that, I want something new in my life that has a purpose, does that make sense?"

"Absolutely," Taylor answered. "As a matter of fact, Pete wondered if I would be interested in overseeing the rebuilding of the towns. I told him he should give Lance this honour; Pete explained Lance would soon be the new Chief of the Similkameen Band and would have enough to keep busy until he was an old man. Then Pete announced he felt it was time he stopped traipsing around the wilderness; he was looking forward to sitting around a warm campfire smoking his pipe and sharing tales with the Elders."

I giggled and visualized Pete puffing on his pipe, while Beau slept curled up beside him on his blanket.

"Pete then told me the reason he asked me to accompany him on his expedition was to find out what my perspective was regarding the deserted towns, and to examine the damage suffered, and if I thought it was feasible to rebuild."

"Did you agree to Pete's request; it sounds like a big job?" I questioned.

"It would keep me busy, and you know I have an interest in environmental renewal. If I decide to take the position, I am going to require an assistant, someone who can go with me on my excursions and keep my sleeping bag warm at night."

I chuckled. "Before you agree to take on the assignment, you should ask Pete if he'll lend you Beau instead to take on your trips."

"That's a terrific idea, having a warm Golden Retriever to cuddle on a cold winter night sounds perfect."

"I'll remember you said that if and when the time comes."

Taylor stood and reached for my hand. "This wooden seat is uncomfortable, let's sit on the porch."

We went outside and we sat side by side, I rested my head on his shoulder.

"You haven't said anything, would you be interested in joining forces with me on Pete's project?"

"I might not be of assistance; I don't know anything about your undertaking."

"I would show you the ropes, it wouldn't take you long to pick it up."

"Taylor, I do appreciate your confidence in me, but right now I cannot give you an answer, I may not be welcomed back in Blackfoot. I've also come to realize I cannot survive on my own at the cabin, especially when the weather turns cold."

"Where do you propose to go?"

"I don't know, I know I've steered clear of Princeton, but that may be my only choice."

"I'm sure Willie will speak to Pete and Mai-Li," Taylor interrupted. "He will let them know the two of you talked. I know you are not ready to pardon Willie; I am not pressuring you, but you seemed more relaxed around him when he was here."

"I was, but that's because you were around. I don't think I could be alone with him, I'm still afraid of him."

"I am aware of that, and so is he. Carlie, a person displaying underlying emotions suffers the most, and it can be an unbearable weight to carry. I need you to reflect on that."

"I understand Taylor, and when the time comes to return to Blackfoot, I'm going back with you. I need to connect with Eddie and find out if he wishes to be with me, in Blackfoot or somewhere else. If he agrees, then he and I will leave and find a new home. I miss him so much."

"He misses you as well and chatters about you constantly. However, taking him from his schoolmates might not be the best decision at this time in his life. He is intelligent and makes top grades, excelling in the sciences and mathematics. He has made friends, something he has never really had a chance to do in his disrupted life."

I smiled and nodded, when Eddie was younger, because of his shyness and insecurities, he relied heavily on Rusty for support and companionship. I was pleased to hear he was maturing and had found a niche in his life.

"It will be men and women like Eddie with these aptitudes and skills," Taylor added, "who will connect with the land and incorporate land-based activities, such as geological field trips or visits to archaeological sites.”

"That sounds so grandiose for such a young boy, what if he doesn't wish to do something like that?"

"We would never push him into anything he was not interested in. I spoke with Eddie, and he was excited when I mentioned Pete's plans. Not only did he show interest, but he asked astute questions, embarrassingly, a couple of which I was not able to answer."

"He was only nine years old when I met him and Rusty, and I was immediately aware of their intelligence."

"Eddie requires the companionship of other children," Taylor added. "And he needs Debbie as much as she needs him. She's a link to his past."

I started crying and wiped my face with the back of my hand. "If I'm not welcome in Blackfoot, then I'll move to Princeton and find work. That way, I won't need to take Eddie out of school, I can work something out so he can visit me in Princeton."

"There's no way I'll let you move to Princeton; Lance was correct when he told you it would be dangerous to stay there on your own. It hasn't been that long since the earthquake, and Princeton's infrastructure and population sustained considerable damage from the earthquake; people are struggling to survive. Many have moved inland and are interested in assisting with the reconstruction of the discarded towns, which would entitle them to ownership to one of the restored homesteads.”

“If Princeton is off the table, then maybe I could go to Kelowna or Vernon.”

“Carlie, that’s just wishful thinking, I imagine most of the interior cities have similar problems, the answer is not returning to urbanization, it’s returning to rural areas and living off the land.”

“I already tried the grid thing, and I blew that,” I muttered. “I can’t earn a living, I can’t take care of myself, and I can’t get my family back.”

Taylor grinned and held me tighter. “You developed the courage to try surviving on your own. We’ll work it out and find a solution. I have no intention of losing you again, and as a last resort, if we can’t work anything out, then Eddie, you and I will leave Blackfoot and find somewhere else to reside.”

“Thank you, Taylor,” I whispered.

“We’ll make it work, now wipe your tears, it’s late and we have a lot of work to do tomorrow.”

Chapter Twenty-three

After our discussion yesterday on the porch, I knew Taylor would stay as long as I needed him, although I was aware of his responsibilities in Blackfoot. Pete expected his return to commence overseeing the restructure of the vacated mining towns.

Taylor's offer that I join him in his new enterprise was appealing, but if I did not reconcile with Willie, it would never happen.

A few days later; we picked the remaining vegetables in the garden and removed Lance's filtration system and stored it in the shed. Taylor spent hours in his wood shop and built a run-in-shed for the corral and repaired two of the porch steps. Later in the day I joined him in the shed. He stood at the counter, distracted, holding a carving of a wooden bear in his hand. He handed it to me, and I smiled. "This is Eddie's, I forgot he lost it, we spent days trying to find it."

Taylor smiled and put it in his pocket. "It fell behind the counter, I'll take it back to him, he can put it on the shelf in his room along with his other treasures."

"Taylor, is Eddie living with you again?"

"When I returned with Pete, I went to the Sih yuan House to get him, and it took him five minutes to pack and haul his belongings back to his bedroom."

"A growing boy needs privacy," I commented. "I'm glad he's back with you. What happened to Squishy?"

"He still has Squishy, he keeps him on his top shelf, along with his books and memories of Rusty. When Willie and I came here, Lance's mother offered to take care of him until we returned. There are more boys closer to his age in the First Nation's Village, he knows them from school."

I nodded, yearning to be with Eddie again.

"And it's not my house," Taylor added. "It's OUR home, mine, yours and Eddie's."

"It will probably be a while before I move back in, I don't imagine I'll be welcomed with open arms."

"Then we'll have to make sure it happens. I'm almost finished in here, give me a hand in cleaning up, then we'll have something to eat."

After lunch, we moved the pile of wood by the firepit into the shed. I knew Taylor's thoughts were in Blackfoot, he was eager to leave, and it was time I let him know what I had decided.

We puttered around the cabin the rest of the afternoon, and I cooked a large supper. Afterwards, we sat outside on the porch. There was a definite disparity in the weather, the mornings were misty, the air was crisper, and the days were shorter. The mountains, shielded by the brilliant hues of the autumn leaves, were breathtaking.

"You know what we need, Taylor?" I announced.

"I'm afraid to ask, although I suspect you're going to enlighten me anyway," he mumbled.

"Rocking chairs, or a hammock; we spend so much time out here, what do you think?"

"Let's add it to our list; it'll be a great project to work on with Eddie the next time we come to the cabin."

I felt a sharp pain in my chest, and I bit my lip.

"Carlie, what's wrong?" Taylor inquired.

I shook my head, rose and headed toward the cabin. He reached for my hand. "I know something's bothering you."

"It's almost a year since we left the meadow," I murmured. "So much has happened since then."

Taylor pulled me close, then whispered, "You're thinking about Rusty?"

I nodded, fighting back tears.

"Carlie, I miss him too, he was a genuine, special boy."

"I know, I talk to him when I'm alone; and I know he senses me. I painted a portrait of him, and I keep it in my backpack."

"That's your way of remembering him. I know Eddie communicates with him all the time as well."

It was as if a door suddenly opened, and all I had to do was walk through. "Taylor, it's time we left. I'll talk to Willie, I know he longs to put this whole mess behind him, as do I. We'll work it out."

"You're determined to do this?"

I nodded. "I know Eddie's safe and well-cared for, but we are his family, and he needs us."

"We're almost finished here at the cabin; I took extra time on it as I want to leave it in half-decent shape."

"Are we coming back?" I enquired.

"I'd enjoy spending time here with the kids during their school breaks or Christmas. I imagine it will be easy to persuade Eddie and Debbie to come; they have some terrific memories of this place and would have a wonderful time."

"That's true; how are we going to convince Debbie to come without Mai-Li."

"Mai-Li must come too."

"That's a lovely idea; except we'll have a full house."

"We've managed before with no problem."

"True, however, things have changed; I don't know where Mai-Li's ten bodyguards would stay."

Taylor snorted. "They're trained soldiers and warriors, and quite capable of surviving anywhere."

"I don't imagine she'll have a lot of time to take holidays; she is running an entire town."

"You're just making excuses," Taylor whispered, as he leaned towards me. "I believe you want me all to yourself."

"Yeah, that's it," I kidded.

I raised my head and stared at the cloudless sky. The moon's silvery reflection illuminated the natural beauty of the landscape. Chirping crickets and the soothing flow of the stream enhanced the peaceful setting. I would miss our chats and tranquil moments on the porch. Not knowing what my future would be added to my anxiety. I sought security and happiness, and the only way I could make that happen was to put aside my anger and negative emotions.

I sighed, and Taylor held me; I turned and looked at him, and he raised his eyebrows waiting for me to share another brilliant idea.

"I wish there was a way we could let travellers who are looking for shelter know they are welcome to utilize the cabin," I voiced. "As long as it's clean when they leave."

"That's a fabulous idea; we could leave a note on the table. It would be a gamble, alternatively, not all people are takers, many appreciate kindness, especially when they are down and out.”

“I was thinking about the time we found the cabin, it was in terrible shape, but it was our salvation.”

“Maybe one day people will realize how lucky and fortunate they are to live in a country that offers so much.”

I shrugged. “Change and progress is slow, and it’s been twenty-four years since the first wildfire in Canada. In 2025 and 2026 there were internal conflicts and wars, economic insecurity, and widespread inflation, causing a worldwide recession.”

“I strongly believe the answer is man must return to the land and come to appreciate nature and what it has to offer,” Taylor whispered.

“That sounds idyllic, and one day that will be the answer. Yet wildfires are a continuous threat, and climate change is a major concern,” I added.

“Climate change and global warming are related, but are separate occurrences,” Taylor continued. “Global warming refers specifically to Earth’s expanding surface temperature due to increased applications of greenhouse gases, powered by human actions, such as burning fossil fuels, deforestation, and industrial processes.”

I did not interrupt; aware he needed no encouragement to continue.

“Climate change,” he declared, “not only incorporates global warming; it also alternates weather patterns, rising sea levels, and severe weather. It's extremely crucial," he advised, "that people recognize the difference between global warming and climate change."

I studied Taylor's face; I missed these interactions with him and Mai-Li when we stayed here at the cabin before arriving at Blackfoot. The wind blew gusts of drifting snow against the windows, and the kids slept comfortably in their bedrolls.

Taylor had a dynamic personality, which Pete homed in on. Taylor's ecological and firsthand experiences played a crucial role in shaping his temperament. With the natural ability to inspire and motivate others he was not afraid to face challenges.

"You've decided to take Pete's offer?" I questioned.

"Unquestionably, I already have. However, you haven't answered me yet, are you interested in joining me?"

"I would enjoy nothing better, once I know my future. I'll have to further my education before I team up with you on your project. As well, I cannot leave Eddie when we have just re-connected with him, not only does he require stability in his life, but he also needs us."

"That's sound advice, Carlie, and works perfectly with my strategies."

I frowned. What was Taylor up to now?

"Before we begin on the project, we need to set up a business. Eddie will be attending school during the day. As well, you might spend some time with the artisans and craftsmen to develop your art. While you're doing that, I'll set up an office. I know there are a few empty offices available at the Sih yuan House. At first there will only be a limited amount of people involved with the project, and I will periodically return to the building sites to check on our progress and solve ongoing issues. There won't be much work done until spring; not until the trails open again, then we'll start construction in earnest. You can manage the office during the day while Eddie's in school."

"Did you arrange this just now?"

"Not all of it, besides, it was only a matter of time before you came around."

"Pretty sure of yourself," I chuckled.

"I know you worship me and yearn to be with me. You're looking for the same thing I am, happiness and a future."

I pressed my head against his chest, then giggled. "Worship might not be the precise word, Taylor."

"Just so you know, I have no intention of moving back into the single men's quarters. You know how much I care about you, how much I love you, and I do not intend to lose you again."

"You won't, I'm not going any place."

"Carlie Fleming, will you marry me?"

I inhaled sharply, lifted my head, and answered, "Yes, I will."

Taylor leaned over and kissed me. I did not know what my future held, however accepting Taylor's proposal felt sincere.

The next morning, we packed our supplies and left. I was surprised when Taylor turned away from the trail and into the bush, taking Lance's hidden shortcut.

Except to rest and water the horses, we stayed near the stream and did not stop until we arrived at a clearing. I assisted Taylor in setting up the tent, then he started a campfire, and I prepared a quick meal. Darkness arrived earlier this time of year, and we decided to retire early, as Taylor was determined to be back on the trail at sunrise.

We laid out the sleeping bags. As the nights were colder, we kept our coats on, using my bag as a cover. Taylor wrapped his arms around me, and I turned and looked at him.

"Remember when we were at the cabin and went moose hunting, we spent the night outside?" I asked.

"I do," he replied.

"It seems as if it was a lifetime ago."

"One of the best hunting trips I'd ever been on."

I laughed. "It was cold and back-breaking work."

"It was the company I was with, I think about it often."

"Me too, those were good times."

"Yes, they were," Taylor yawned. "Now close your eyes, we're leaving early tomorrow. I intend to arrive in Blackfoot before sunset."

The next morning, we were on the trail early. We stopped to rest and water the horses and ate while we travelled.

Late in the afternoon, we reached the Similkameen River; and soon arrived at the bridge. We stopped and waited, as we knew the residents of Blackfoot would be aware of our arrival.

"Taylor, Carlie," a voice called behind us. I turned and watched as Lance, riding Ginger, galloped towards us. When he reached us, he dismounted and approached Thunder, who was trying to greet Ginger.

"Thunder," Lance ordered sharply.

Thunder immediately settled down, Lance smiled and reached up to take my hand and stopped. He looked at me, then turned and faced Taylor.

"You have found each other again."

"All is well with you?" Taylor questioned.

I understood what Taylor was asking Lance, and I held my breath.

"Yes, it's good, and as it should be. I am delighted for both of you."

"Thank you, Lance," I whispered.

Lance nodded and rubbed Thunder's muzzle. When the opportunity arose, I would talk to him. He was a friend, and I owed him my thanks for his support when I was alone and needed help. I was relieved there was no animosity between him and Taylor.

"How long have you been back?" Taylor said to Lance.

"I just returned; Grandfather's keeping me busy; there is much to learn."

"It is wonderful the Similkameen Band will soon have a new and wise chief to lead them."

Lance accepted Taylor's compliment. "My wandering days are ending, it is time to consider the futures of our people. Follow me back to the Village, I'm sure you're both tired and hungry. When you have rested, we will discuss Grandfather's project."

Taylor nodded, and Lucy and Thunder fell in stride behind Ginger. When we arrived, we dismounted, two men approached and took the horses' reins.

"We'll leave your supplies inside the hall, Taylor," one of them mentioned.

Taylor nodded his thanks, and the three of us strolled to the campfire. Pete watched as we approached, took a puff on his pipe, then lowered his head in greeting. Beau barrelled towards us, almost knocking me over. Taylor caught me before I fell, and Pete chuckled. Lance sat down next to Pete, leaving room for Beau, and gestured for us to join him.

Food and drinks were passed around and while we ate, Lance opened the conversation. "Grandfather exchanged his ideas with me regarding the reconstruction of the abandoned mining towns, and he also informed me he had invited you to head the project.”

“He did, and I gratefully accepted. The wildfires have decelerated, there’s more rain, which is a dual benefit in our favour. In fact, I’m trying to convince Carlie to join me.”

“You mean to apply her artistic talents in promoting the project?”

“As well as her organizational skills, there will be times I will be required to return to the sites, and she can keep matters progressing in Blackfoot when I’m absent.”

“That would work, what are your thoughts on this, Carlie?” Lance queried.

“I agreed, if I am allowed to remain in Blackfoot, and I can start again with my art instructions. However, my main priority is Eddie, Taylor told me he enjoys school and is making excellent grades.”

Lance pointed towards a tidy bungalow located next to the tree line. I stood and headed towards the trail that separated the centre of the Village from the housing units.

A smiling middle-aged woman stood in the doorway. She laughed when Eddie ran past her and threw his arms around my neck. I hugged him, holding him close. “Carlie,” he sobbed. “How come you were gone so long? No-one would tell me when you were coming back.”

“Eddie, I am so sorry, I had a few things to sort out before I returned,” I answered.

He smiled and nodded eagerly, then noticed Taylor and Lance sitting at the campfire. He pulled me towards the two men, but I stopped him and said, "Isn't there someone you should thank first."

Eddie sheepishly lowered his head, gripped my hand, and raced back to the house. Charity was still standing in the doorway. "Mrs. Johnson, thank you for letting me stay with you, and taking care of me."

"You're welcome, Eddie. I enjoyed your company."

Then she turned and faced me. "You must be Carlie?"

"Yes, I am, and I'm glad to meet you, Mrs. Johnson. I have so much to thank you for, not only caring for Eddie, but for a bag of seeds that turned out to be extremely useful, and your delicious Bannock, which didn't last too long."

Mrs. Johnson chuckled. "You're welcome, call me Charity; Mrs. Johnson makes me sound old."

I giggled, I thought how appropriate her name was.

Eddie impatiently pulled me towards the Village. "You better take him to the Village," Charity chuckled. "I think there's someone else Eddie wants to greet."

I turned to leave when Eddie abruptly stopped. "Oh, my clothes and stuff, I forgot them."

"Eddie, I'll give them to Lance, and he can bring them to you later, once you're settled," Charity explained.

When we arrived at the campfire, he ran towards Taylor, who hugged him tightly.

"Hey guy, I missed you," Taylor declared. "I'm sorry I took so long coming back."

"It's okay," Eddie affirmed, as he turned and looked at me. "You had to take care of Carlie. Can we go home now?"

I realized how much the two of them meant to me. They were my family; and if possible, I vowed I would never be separated from them again.

"Can we go home now?" Eddie requested.

"Soon Eddie, but right now, Carlie and I have something to share with you."

"Taylor, not now," I interrupted, looking nervously as the people sitting or standing around the campfire.

"No time like the present."

All conversation stopped, everyone waited patiently. I would have a long discussion with Taylor later, he knew how much I disliked sharing personal information with strangers.

"Carlie and I are engaged; we're getting married."

Eddie's mouth flew open, then he cheered, and jumped up and down in excitement. Soon we were surrounded by well-wishers, who congratulated us, and wondered if we had set a date.

Lance shook Taylor's hand. "Congratulations, although I can't say I'm surprised." Then he approached and kissed me. "I never had a chance, did I?"

"You were a close second," I replied. "Are we okay?"

"Always," he concurred, then turned and faced Taylor. "We need to talk, bring Carlie and Eddie with you."

We dogged Lance to his mother's house, who was waiting patiently at the door. Spotting Eddie, she mentioned there was milk and cookies in the kitchen. Eddie looked at me and tightened his grip.

"Eddie, I'll be right here with Taylor and Lance, and when we leave, I'll come get you."

Eddie nodded and trailed Charity into the kitchen. I understood his anxiety and instability; we were together since I rescued him and Rusty at Little Mountain. Losing his brother, then being separated from me and Taylor, only added to his insecurity.

Lance opened a door on the far side of the room; he entered and we followed him inside. There was a wooden desk, an armchair, and a big, comfortable sofa touching the far wall.

"Is this Pete's office?" I asked.

Lance shook his head. "No, Grandfather has no interest in indoor workplaces; he finds them confining and is happiest when he's rambling through the forest, or when he's alone at his cabin. When he seeks company, he returns to the Village to lounge around the campfire to share his adventures and traditional stories with the Elders."

"When you stayed with me at the cabin, I got the impression you were similar to your grandfather, at peace when surrounded by nature and removed from civilization."

"I have been compared to him; however, I am no longer an adolescence, I am a man, and it's time to find my purpose in life. The people of Blackfoot must build and develop relationships to the natural world and with the land; and interact with the environment and our community. It is essential we bring back qualities that have been lost, restore the land to its natural state."

"You know Carlie and I are behind you all the way," Taylor advised, turning towards me.

"I realize I can rely on both of you. Projects and activities on how to support a deeper understanding of the land and the alterations that have resulted from climate change are being introduced into our community, as well as taught in the schools. We need to allocate more resources, implement more inclusive practices, launch new projects, and with time, improvements will become evident."

"However, this is not what I wish to discuss," Lance interrupted, looking at me. "I met with Mai-Li yesterday, and she knows you're back and requested I ask you and

Taylor to meet with her tomorrow morning as she would like to talk with the two of you."

Taylor watched me closely. My mind raced, I was not prepared to face Mai-Li, not if she planned to take Eddie from me again. He reached over and took my hand. "Carlie, I know what's on your mind, I don't believe Mai-Li wants to discuss Eddie, I'm sure she knows he is safe with us."

"She's wants to discuss Willie with me," I mumbled.

"Carlie, may I interrupt," Lance requested. "I spoke to Willie when he returned earlier and before he left for Princeton to find his mother. He mentioned he talked to you and had apologized. He also informed me you did not absolve him and would let him know when you were ready to do so. He seemed pleased with your response. This was a huge step for him, and he needs closure, as do you."

Taylor watched both of us and interrupted. "Lance, I'm sorry Willie dragged you into this, it's not your worry, you have enough on your mind."

"Willie did not start the conversation, I did. I was aware of what happened; Carlie and I discussed it when we were at the cabin."

Taylor stiffened, and his face flushed red with anger.

"This is my problem," I interrupted, fearing an altercation between Lance and Taylor. "I will take care of it. If Willie and I can't sort it out, and Mai-Li does not change her mind, then I will leave and take Eddie with me."

"I will leave with you," Taylor added. "I have no intention of losing my family again."

I stood abruptly and headed towards the door; followed closely by Taylor.

"Stop" a commanding voice ordered. "Sit down, both of you."

Lance was standing behind his desk, and from the look on his face, he demanded immediate acquiescence from both of us. Taylor and I returned to our seats.

"I am sorry I raised my voice; this matter will be settled now. Neither of you will be leaving Blackfoot, you are part of our community, and your significant expertise and abilities are in demand. Mai-Li is aware of what occurred between Carlie and Willie at the cabin, she met with him prior to his leaving for Princeton, and a decision was made. She will discuss it with you when you meet."

I trembled and lifted my head. Would this nightmare never end?

"Alright Lance, we'll join you tomorrow at Mai-Li's," Taylor confirmed. "We are not sure where we stand regarding the house, can we set up our tent next to the Village?"

"If I agreed to that my mother would disown me. She has prepared the guest room for Carlie, and you and Eddie can share my room, I will spend the night with Grandfather in the Village. Your supplies have been dropped off here; you'll have everything you need."

I retired early and slept through the night. I woke with a start when I picked up the sound of voices and laughter; I dressed quickly and strode to the kitchen. Pete, Charity, Lance, Taylor, and Eddie were seated around a large table; I slid into an empty chair beside Taylor.

Everybody simultaneously called "morning," and I nodded. Charity removed a mug from the cupboard and filled it with coffee. She placed it in front of me and handed me a bowl of liquid honey. "I am aware you can't start your day without coffee," she mentioned.

I scowled and looked at Lance. He grinned, kept his head lowered and speared a piece of bacon.

"She's grouchy if she doesn't get her coffee," Eddie shared with everyone. "When we were walking to the Interior, it got really bad when all we had was chicory."

Everyone burst out laughing, and I joined in. After we ate, I assisted Charity in clearing the table and washing the dishes. The men were in the living room and when we joined them, I apologized to Lance for my appearance as all I currently owned were jeans and a tee shirt.

"I'm sure Mai-Li will excuse you, however, I on the other hand, have an image to uphold. You will notice I'm dressed in my best buckskin shirt and pants."

"Aren't they the same clothes you wore all the time you were at the cabin?" I asked nonchalantly.

Lance chuckled, and Taylor frowned.

Charity scoffed and wagged her finger at Lance. "Don't be late for your appointment, Eddie can stay with us; I'm joining Grandfather at the stables, one of the mares is ready to foal."

"Can I go with them, can I, can I," Eddie pleaded. "Please, please."

"If Mrs. Johnson says you can," I answered.

"Of course he can," she replied.

Charity, Pete, and Eddie left and headed towards the barn. Lance, Taylor, and I strolled over the bridge, then travelled towards the Sih yuan House. Two guards were waiting at the entrance; we paced behind them and entered the room where we first met Mai-Li's grandparents when we arrived in Blackfoot. An elegant, stunning woman dressed in an exquisite silk gown sat at the table. When she saw us, she rose and glided towards us.

"Carlie," Mai-Li said, as she faced me. "It is pleasant to see you again. I hope you are well."

The last time we met, we separated under strained circumstances, and I found it difficult to respond. "I am, thank you Mai-Li."

She faced Taylor and greeted him. "Taylor, I am thankful you are here, and may

I congratulate you and Carlie on your wedding announcement."

"Thank you, Mai-Li, pleasant news travels swiftly in Blackfoot."

Mai-Li smiled and bowed her head in acquiescence. Lance chuckled, and Mai-Li approached him; he leaned over and kissed her. I gasped, a stunned look on my face.

"Come sit at the table, tea and appetizers will be served shortly," Mai-Li announced. "I imagine Charity cooked a huge breakfast, however I'm sure there's room for dessert."

I moved towards the table, Mai-Li and Lance sat on one side and Taylor and I sat across from them.

"Lance and I have been dating since he returned from the cabin," Mai-Li announced, noticing my reaction. "We've been working collectively on valuable issues, and it didn't take us long to discover how much we had in common."

I thought about it, and realized they were a perfect match, both held esteemed positions, and their main priorities were Blackfoot and its people.

Mai-Li rose and stepped over to the window and looked outside. "Nature has so much to offer; before we can return to the land, we must teach interested inhabitants how to homestead and grow their own produce. As well, healthy lifestyle alterations must be encouraged. We must return to a simpler way of life. The best way to successfully achieve this is by spending time with our families, to show respect, be considerate of others and support those in need."

I sat rooted, absorbing Mai-Li's words. She turned and faced Lance.

"Recovery of the Earth's natural resources is only a part of the solution," Lance informed. "Environmental recovery is also crucial, and before we can make that happen, wildlife must return, we require clean water in the streams and healthy ecosystems. Due to climate changes, people are leaving the cities and moving farther inland or migrating to northern realms. We must discover how to set up multi-cultural towns and villages. Grandfather's dream of rebuilding abandoned homesteads and towns is part of the solution."

The silence in the room was overpowering. I absorbed Mai-Li and Lances' wise portents. Are we running out of natural resources, are we running out of time? The Earth has given us all we need, now it's our turn to give back.

"Carlie, and Taylor" Mai-Li intervened. "Lance and I must apologize to both of you. When we started spending time together, we soon realized our interests and concerns were the same, the residents of Blackfoot must share their abilities and knowledge to improve the lives of the Princeton residents. Pete and my grandparents have been researching these issues for years. Taylor, you became aware of them when you joined Pete on his expedition."

Taylor nodded and took my hand and squeezed it. At that moment, I realized how unfair I had been to him, and promised I would keep an open mind.

"Carlie, before we begin, there's something I want to discuss with you," Mai-Li remarked. "When Pete requested Taylor join his expedition, Taylor made an impulsive decision. You were indisposed at the time, and he asked me to let you know he was leaving with Pete and he had no idea when they would return. I was overwhelmed with everything happening here, I neglected to inform you. I want to apologise; I don't want to lose your friendship."

"I'm as guilty as you, Mai-Li; I wouldn't listen to Taylor when he tried to recount what really happened, I was just so furious at the time. I want to stay in contact, can we put it behind us."

"Yes, we can, and we will," she replied. "Thank you."

"You can forgive me later, when we are alone," Taylor whispered in my ear.

Mai-Li wagged her finger at Taylor to behave.

"Now, the issue at hand, consider what I have to say, then it can be discussed. Willie visited with me before he left to go to Princeton. He told me he conversed with you, and although some of the tension was lifted, you were still conflicted, which I appreciated. When I issued my ultimatum for you to leave Blackfoot, you were distressed and angry, and I confess I spent many restless nights deliberating over it."

"It was the only decision you could have made, Mai-Li," I answered. "When Willie talked to me, I knew it was time to move ahead."

"It took courage, for both of you, and a solution can be reached. It is time you returned to Blackfoot, and you and Eddie returned to your home. Taylor can stay with Lance until after the wedding."

Taylor scowled and grunted, and Lance hooted. "Have you and Carlie set a date yet?"

I shook my head, and Taylor answered abruptly. "We will as soon as possible."

Mai-Li poked Lance's rib drawing his attention. "Willie inquired if he could bring his mother to Blackfoot; she is not well, and he has sworn to take care of her. Although she left when he was just a young boy, when he found her, she recognized him immediately. Pete and I discussed it and agreed, the responsibility of caring for someone is exactly what Willie requires. Carlie, are you comfortable with this?"

I nodded and reached over and took Taylor's hand. Two graceful women, carrying trays, entered, glided to the table, and set them down. Mai-Li thanked them, they bowed and left. "Help yourself to tea and refreshments," she offered.

We chatted and visited awhile, sharing old memories; there was a knock at the door, and Mai-Li's grandparents entered. They approached me and asked after my health. Mai-Li told them Taylor, and I were engaged to be married, and they bowed and congratulated us.

"It is marvellous you have returned," Grandmother announced. "We miss Eddie. However, there's someone here who wants to see you."

"CARLEEEEEE," a shrill voice echoed around the room. I chuckled as I watched Debbie barrel towards me, Kim Lee, Debbie's nursemaid in close pursuit. The excited girl stopped abruptly, and I waited patiently for her to make the first move.

"Can I hug you?" I spoke. Debbie nodded and wrapped her arms around my waist. I marvelled at her transformation, she was calm, or as calm as Debbie could be.

"OH, MY GOOOSHH, IT'S TAYLOR," she squealed when she realized who was sitting next to me. She released me and Taylor opened his arms, she leaned against him, hugging him cautiously.

During the entire reunion, Kim Lee wrung her hands, and when she tried to extricate Taylor, I waited for Debbie's reaction.

"Kim Lee, it's alright," Mai-Li interrupted. "She hasn't seen Carlie or Taylor in a long time."

The loyal nursemaid nodded, then sat at the table. I didn't begrudge what would be in store for her later after they left, even though the improvement in Debbie's demeanour was incredible.

Debbie patted Taylor's cheek, then patted my arm, and joined Kim Lee at the table.

"Can I have a cookie?" she asked, as she spotted the refreshment tray.

"Just one," Kim Lee answered, "You don't want to ruin your lunch."

"Yes, I do," she declared, as she took Kim Lee's hand and left the room.

"It was enjoyable seeing you both again," Mai-Li's grandmother began. "However, our lunch will soon be prepared, we must not be late, or Debbie will give us a time out."

Taylor and I laughed as they turned and left the room and Mai-Li's grandfather chuckled at Debbie's' response to Kim Lee regarding the cookie. It was evident they enjoyed spending time with the young girl and accepted her as one of their own.

I was reminded of the continuous struggles Mai-Li underwent with Debbie on our trek to the Interior. What Debbie had been missing in her life was stability and understanding.

We sat and chatted awhile and discussed the wedding. Mai-Li felt it would lift the spirits of the people in Blackfoot.

There was a lull in the conversation, and Mai-Li cleared her throat. She looked at Taylor, and he nodded.

"Carlie," he began. "Mai-Li and I have something we'd like to discuss with you. It's about Rusty."

I twitched and took a deep breath.

"After we share our thoughts, you can let us know how you feel."

Apprehensive and uneasy, I nodded in agreement.

"Mai-Li has offered to send her guards to the meadow where we buried Rusty. We wish to exhume his body and bring him to Blackfoot to bury him in the cemetery."

Taylor hesitated when he noticed the look on my face. I inhaled sharply, overcome with emotion. I began to tremble, and he took me in his arms and waited on my answer.

"I'm not sure what to say, I strongly feel we should discuss this matter with Eddie and find out if he agrees." I murmured.

"Carlie, I've discussed this matter previously with Eddie," Taylor remarked. "He said he would be okay if we did, but first I had to let you know and find out how you feel about it. He's very aware of the close connection you had with Rusty."

I wiped the tears from my face and faced Mai-Li. "When will you send your guards, it'll take a while to trek to the meadow and return."

"We have horses and supplies, and my guards are well-trained, and I do not foresee any problems. I'll send them after your wedding. When the time is right, we'll have an interment and celebrate Rusty's life. It will be closure for all of us, especially Eddie, having his twin brother close by."

I stood and moved towards Mai-Li. Then I embraced and thanked her. "My little boy will be coming home."

Lance, Taylor, and I left not long afterwards, and we returned to the Village. Taylor and Lance joined Pete at the campfire, and I went across the road to Charity's home. I knocked on the door, and the door was flung open.

"Come in Carlie, our home is open to everyone, you do not need to knock. How was your visit with Mai-Li?"

"We chatted and became reacquainted with Mai-Li's grandparents. Is Eddie here?"

Hearing our voices, Eddie scrambled down the hall. "Is everything okay?" he inquired.

"Everything is fine, Taylor and I just saw Debbie, she was excited seeing both of us. She wondered where you were, and if you want, you can go there tomorrow to play with her for a while."

"Carlie, I don't play with Debbie anymore, I'm too old. I just visit with her."

"I'm sorry, I didn't know that. I won't forget next time."

Eddie nodded, then looked around the room. "Where's the guys?"

"At the Village, you can join ...." I've never seen Eddie move so quickly, the door was slammed shut before I finished answering. Eddie was growing up so fast, and it wouldn't be long before he was a teenager.

Charity stood in the kitchen doorway and laughed. "He's incredibly special and a joy to have around. He's extremely attached to you; talked about you non-stop. He told me how he and his brother Rusty met you and Taylor."

"Eddie was mature for his age; Rusty kept us entertained and on our toes."

I went with Charity to the kitchen; she poured me a cup of tea, then we moved outside to the back porch and sat in comfortable lounge chairs. She watched me closely, then cleared her throat. "After Lance returned with Pete, he told me how close you two became when he was at the cabin, then he admitted he thought he might be in love with you."

My face reddened, and I lowered my face, at a loss for words.

"Have I overstepped my boundaries?" she inquired when I didn't answer.

I shook my head, "When he told me, I was conflicted, but he had to return to Blackfoot right away. That was when I realized it was Taylor I loved. When we arrived in Blackfoot, we ran into Lance, who immediately realized how much Taylor and I cared for each other."

I reached over and took Charity's hands. "I am so delighted he found Mai-Li; they share the same interests and are a formidable couple. Their main priority is the welfare of Blackfoot and its residents."

"Thank you for being so candid with me," Charity responded. "Carlie, if you don't mind me changing the topic, did you receive Mai-Li's decision on your future living conditions."

"I'm sorry, I should have mentioned it earlier. Eddie and I will be moving back into the house, and Taylor will stay in the Village until after the wedding."

"If you are agreeable, I would be delighted to assist in organizing your wedding."

"Thank you, Charity, I would have been lost doing it on my own. I imagine wedding ceremonies in Blackfoot are unlike the ones I attended growing up in Vancouver."

Later that day, Taylor, Eddie, and I returned to the house. The first item that caught my eye was the wooden necklace Taylor carved me; he picked it up and handed it to me, and I placed it in my pocket.

Our supplies were dropped off earlier, and soon everything was unpacked. The fridge was stocked with food; the lawn was mowed, and the flowers watered. Taylor decided to leave most of his clothes and personal articles and take only what was necessary to stay in the Village. He spent most of the day with us and did not join Pete until later in the day. Eddie's room was returned to its original tidy condition. He stored his books on his shelves, and Squishy was propped against a pillow on the spare bunkbed. I retrieved the portrait I painted of Rusty and gave it to him. Taylor found a nail and a hammer, and they hung it on the wall next to Rusty's compass. Taylor returned my portrait I painted of him to its rightful place above the bed in the main bedroom.

Days later, I strolled to the Village to visit with Charity and was surprised when I spotted Willie conversing with Pete. An elderly woman clung to his arm, she was stout, attractive, with chestnut brown eyes and brown hair streaked with white. Stiff backed and severe looking, she shook my hand when Willie introduced his mother and I recalled he told us he found her in Princeton on the streets, struggling to survive. Pete pointed to one of the empty homes and told Willie he and his mother could reside there if they wished. It was evident she was not well, and the long hike from Princeton must have been arduous. Pete suggested Willie take her to the healing centre. I later discovered her name was Eunice.

After Willie dropped his mother off at the healing centre, he joined us and announced he had news to share. I made tea, and we sat outside on the porch. Willie mentioned his mother was hesitant in coming to Blackfoot as she felt she would not be accepted. He convinced her that would not be the case, and she was not well enough to survive on her own. She finally agreed, although the trek from Princeton was long and gruelling, and they stopped often to rest.

"However, that's not what I want to disclose. I connected with some people I met earlier while searching for my mother. The name Lars was mentioned, and when I realized it was him, I warned them to be cautious, as he would not hesitate to steal their weapons and anything of value. One of them told me that's exactly what happened, a fight ensued, and Lars was killed. The police were updated; there were no repercussions. Most of the people who are homeless struggle to survive, and Lars suffered the ultimate price."

None of us answered, each of us confronted Lars's wrath in the past, it was time to put it behind us and move on.

I cleared my throat, faced Willie, and told him I forgave him. I did not wish to carry this burden any longer, and it was time to let go. Willie lowered his head, "Thank you, Carlie, I know how stressful this has been for you. I spoke to my mother about what happened; she told me she worried I was following in my father's footsteps, as he was a bitter and abusive man, which was why she left him. She hoped I would set this matter right, as she knew there was goodness in me, and she did not intend to lose me again."

"Let her know when she improves that we've discussed and resolved this matter, and perhaps you could let Pete know the outcome as well, although I'm strongly aware he's privy to everything that happens in Blackfoot." Willie nodded and lowered his head. "Carlie, it will take me a long time to forgive myself for what I did. I know I carried a lot of resentment at that time, but it's not an excuse or a reason for doing what I did. Even now I find it challenging to make amends. Communicating with Pete and my mother has provided the emotional support I require."

Taylor sat still while Willie and I talked. He reached over and took my hand, then squeezed Willie's arm. "It's a step in the right direction for both of you."

Chapter Twenty-Four

The opening of the office building was crucial for Blackfoot; and those with spare time worked on the project. It was decided construction of the deserted towns and mines would begin in early spring, and the preliminary work at the sites could be started before the paths and roadways were buried under snow.

Lance suggested Taylor and I marry prior to that time, and when Taylor gave me the news, I ran all the way to Charity's house to disclose the appalling news. She laughed and gave me a glass of water. "Sit down, drink this, and take a deep breath."

"What am I going to do, we can't put on a wedding in a few weeks."

"Nonsense, Blackfoot is not a big town. Once you have chosen an officiate, we'll check at the Community Hall and set a date. Everyone attending the event will pitch in and bring food, which leaves the ceremony."

"Oh no, who's going to marry us?" I wondered. "Lance is the best man, Willie is the groomsman, Mai-Li is my maid of honour and you're my bridesmaid, Debbie's the flower girl and Eddie's the ring bearer. There's no-one left."

"None of the people you've listed have the power to marry you in any event, especially Debbie or Eddie," Charity smiled. "Only Pete or Mai-Li's grandmother have that honour and either one would be pleased to officiate. Discuss this with Taylor tonight, choose who you would like to perform the ceremony, then let me know and I'll talk to them. Then we can set a date at the Community Hall."

"What if they say no?"

"I don't think that's a worry, now relax, everything will work out fine."

"I've never organized a wedding before."

"I didn't notice," Charity chuckled.

"I don't know a lot of people in Blackfoot, who should I invite?"

"It isn't necessary to have a guest list, once word gets out, anyone living in Blackfoot and in the surrounding area are welcome to attend. It doesn't take long for information to spread when a public event is scheduled."

Charity was true to her word and pitched in to help. She took me to a small shop, having the impressive name of Urban Clothing and Gift Boutique. It was located across the bridge and close to the medical centre. She introduced me to the owner, Martha Pedersen, a pleasant hardy woman with blonde hair, blue eyes, and a permanent smile. When we mentioned I was looking for a wedding dress, Martha's face lit up, and she gleefully pointed to a back room, which held rows of women's clothing and personal items. We laughed, chatted, and ribald quips regarding my upcoming nuptials were shared. I had no idea what I was looking for, then I found a graceful and sophisticated ankle-length white cotton dress, with a low neckline and white shoes to match. I tried them on, and both fit perfectly. When I inquired about the price, Martha informed me money was worthless in Blackfoot, which is why they used the barter system. I panicked when I realized I owned nothing of value.

Charity took my arm and guided me around the store and pointed to the articles on display; hand-made jewellery, dried flower arrangements, shellac animal's bones, wreaths made from nuts, dried flowers and acorns, owls made from tree bark and pinecones.

"Carlie, everything a person owns is worth something, either to them or to someone else. What is it you have that might be of value?"

I shrugged, then I knew what Charity meant. I returned to the sales lady and questioned if she might be interested in trading for paintings or sketches.

Martha's head shot up, and she wanted to know what I painted. I told her landscapes, flowers, trees, portraits, abandoned towns and rustic cabins, and I recently drafted articles and portrayed pictures of wildfires. I advised her I began my training with the Blackfoot artisans and craftsmen and would bring some of my artwork tomorrow for her to look at.

Early the next morning, carrying two bags full of my artwork, Charity and I returned to the shop. I reached to turn the handle when Charity stopped me and whispered. "Before we go in remember bartering is a skill, so pay attention and listen closely."

Martha was waiting at the counter, and she carefully examined each of them; she gleefully traded one of my smaller wildflower paintings for the shoes. Then the bargaining began in earnest when she spotted the larger landscape that I painted of the Tulameen Falls. It took Charity close to an hour before she struck a bargain, and it didn't take me long to realize not only was she in her element; she was enjoying herself. The painting was exchanged for the dress and an exquisite flower headband. I would be forever grateful to Charity and decided to give her one of my paintings as a gift.

I was thrilled as I returned home with my treasures; the first thing I did was hide my purchases in the closet, as Taylor dropped by every night for supper. After we ate, and as school recently reopened after the Thanksgiving holiday, we questioned Eddie about the subjects he was taking, his teachers and his classmates.

Then I discussed the matter of choosing a marriage officiant, either Pete or Mai-Li's grandmother. We included Eddie in our discussion, and it was decided to ask Pete first. Taylor advised he would meet with him tomorrow and would let me know his answer.

When approached, Pete said he would be honoured to officiate at the wedding. I let Charity know, and she smiled, which made me wonder if she already knew Pete would be asked and what his answer would be. We went to the Community Hall and booked a date.

The days passed quickly, and now that I was aware of the barter system, I found stores that traded blankets, comforters and towels, and another dishes and kitchenware. It did not take Eddie and Taylor long to notice the additions I made in the house, and I told them about the barter system, which of course, Taylor was aware of. Then I mentioned my paintings and sketches were in demand, which I used to trade.

I returned often to Martha's store, and we soon became close acquaintances. I checked Eddie's clothes and discovered he had gone through a growing spurt; I traded a few of my paintings for pants, a shirt, a jacket, and shoes. I also got him underwear, socks, winter leggings, and a fall jacket.

I talked to Eddie and requested he go through his clothes and give me anything that did not fit anymore. The next morning,

I found a bag of clothes in the kitchen, and I spent the day washing them, then I trudged down to Martha's and traded them for items I wanted for the house. Before I left, I opened a trading account.

Eddie was excited with his new wardrobe, and when Taylor arrived that night, he dragged him into his bedroom and showed him his new clothes. Later that night, after Eddie did his homework and went to bed, Taylor asked me what I used to barter with.

"My paintings," I answered. "For some reason, they're in demand." Then I asked Taylor if he had appropriate attire for the wedding, and he informed me Lance had taken him to a men's clothing store, and he found everything he needed.

"What did you use to barter with?" I asked.

"Lance covered it for me; I'll repay him when I can."

I told Taylor to follow me to the storage room. My paintings were piled against the wall and stored in boxes and cupboards. "I don't want to start our marriage owing anything, so take what you need to trade for your clothes."

Taylor smiled and took me in his arms. "Thank you, I'll talk to the clerk tomorrow."

I hoped my paintings would last for a while, and there was a demand for them in Blackfoot, as I had no idea how much time I would have to work on my artwork once work began on the project.

That night after supper, I told Eddie and Taylor about the new account. I told Eddie when he outgrew his clothes or shoes, I would take him to the shop as he was old enough now to choose his own outfits. He thanked me, and I waited for his hug. He strode towards the bookshelf, chose a book, turned and strutted into this bedroom. The look of disappointment on my face was a giveaway, and Taylor pulled me close. "He's growing up Carlie, it's not cool for a boy his age to hug or kiss his parents, as for all intents and purposes, that's who we are to him."

Taylor and I discussed the barter system and its advantages and disadvantages for isolated villages where paper currency was not available. We arrived at a mutual consensus; the system would work if people were honest and fair with each other.

Time passed quickly, and the wedding day arrived. I trekked to Charity's house early in the morning. She poured me a cup of coffee, and we rolled our hair in curlers.

The first item on our agenda was a wedding bouquet which we made from colourful autumn wildflowers. There were asters, hawk wood, forget-me-nots, blanket flowers, and yellow daisies, which grew in abundance in the area.

Mai-Li and Debbie arrived; I had left it up to Mai-Li to choose their own outfits for the wedding. Her silk knee length dress was vibrant red, and Debbie was outfitted in a frilly red dress to match. When Kim Lee tried to dress Debbie for the wedding, pandemonium erupted, and Mai-Li was called to Debbie's room to explain why she had to wear a pretty dress and have her hair brushed and curled. When she was told Eddie would be there and dressed up too, she settled down.

We slipped into Charity's bedroom to dress. She reached inside her closet and removed a buckskin dress adorned with quillwork. It was exquisite, and I asked her if she made it. She replied that the women in her band did all their own sewing, and I remembered Lance's outfit and assumed that was one of her creations.

"I was never taught how to sew," I confessed. "We bought most of our clothing from stores."

"Did your mother not sew?"

I shook my head, invoking latent memories. "My mother was a businesswoman; she and my father were seismologists and worked at the Vancouver University."

"You must be incredibly proud of your heritage; I have always respected married women who were educated and worked at a demanding job yet managed to take care of her home and care for her children too."

"I wish she and my father were here today," I murmured.

"They are, Carlie."

"Sometimes I can sense their presence."

"They are letting you know they are watching over you." Charity answered softly.

"I've never discussed this with anyone before, however, for some reason, I'm comfortable mentioning it to you."

"Our people have a different outlook on death, when a person dies the entire community mourns, and nature provides the comfort and closure needed."

"There's so much to learn, not only about your people but Mai-Li's people as well."

"You will in time, for now, it's time we got dressed," Charity announced.

I removed the curlers and brushed my hair; then I put on my wedding dress. I left my hair down and pinned on the headband. I exclaimed when I saw multi-coloured wildflowers intertwined around the band.

"Charity, did you do this?"

"I did," she confessed. "Is it alright?"

I nodded. "The flowers match the wedding bouquet, they're perfect."

I then retrieved my shoes and put them on. I wondered how comfortable I would be wearing them, as the only footwear I wore since the tsunami was my hiking boots.

I stared at my reflection in the mirror. "Is my neckline too low?"

"Carlie, you're gorgeous," Charity uttered. "I don't believe anyone is going to complain about your dress, especially Taylor."

Charity finished dressing, then wove feathers into her long-braided hair.

We joined Mai-Li and Debbie in the living room. When Debbie saw me, she raced over and gripped me around my waist.

"Carlie, I like your pretty dress, and flower hat."

"Thank you, Debbie, and you're very pretty, you look like a princess."

"Yes, I do," she answered smugly.

Suddenly, she turned and faced Mai-Li, who raised her eyebrows. Debbie slowly lowered her head, then turned and looked back at me. "Carlie, you are awfully pretty too."

"Thank you, Debbie."

"But you still don't look like a princess," she muttered under her breath.

I covered my mouth, controlling my laughter, Charity chuckled, and Mai-Li rolled her eyes.

"Where's Kim Lee?" I enquired.

"She's taking a break; I brought Debbie with me to give Kim Lee a chance to put on her ceremony robe. She'll meet us at the Community Hall."

"She's doing a fantastic job with Debbie?"

"She is, I don't know how I would cope without her; I made Debbie my responsibility when I found her at Little Mountain, although with my current schedule, I've come to rely on Kim Lee for so much. Regrettably, she is getting too old to be Debbie's constant caregiver."

"It is a worry, Mai-Li, nevertheless, you and Lance will work it out."

"Come on people," Charity announced. "It's time to go."

We headed towards the door, suddenly Charity turned and ran into the kitchen, returning with the bouquet. "After all that work, and I almost forgot it."

We strolled through the Village, crossed the bridge, and headed to the Hall. I rolled the hem of my dress around my arm, terrified I would step on it and trip. (I have been known to do that at times).

We eventually arrived at the Hall, the surrounding garden was a balanced blend of trees and vibrant autumn flowers, while the soft murmur of a nearby brook mingled with the chirping birds and the rustle of leaves. On the far side of the yard was a tarp with an enormous barbecue underneath. Smoke filtered upwards and I inhaled the aroma of smoked meat and fish.

Charity guided us to the door, and a group of giggling women ushered us into a massive room. There were rows of tables set up with colourful tablecloths, dishes, and cutlery, as was the head table, which faced the room. I spotted a half-open door, and inside the room was a refrigerator and a freezer, and numerous shelves loaded with supplies.

I kept an eye on Debbie; huge crowds intimidated her, and if she had a melt-down it could take hours to quieten her. Mai-Li must have had similar thoughts, as she gestured for Kim Lee, who waited by one of the tables, to join us. They talked quietly, then the faithful nanny took Debbie's hand and headed towards the back door.

"Can we go to the brook?" Debbie asked.

Mai-Li noticed the look on my face, and chuckled. "She's a lot better around water now, Carlie. Kim-Lee always carries cookies or crackers in her pocket."

Charity motioned Mai-Li and me over. "It's been decided to have the ceremony outside; it's a beautiful day. Are you okay with that Carlie?"

"You are the marriage organizer, and I trust you explicitly."

"Except for Debbie and Eddie, the rest of the wedding party will go straight outside to the podium. Carlie, hide in the back room, and Pete will join you. We can't let Taylor see you."

I nodded and headed to the back, the door was ajar, and I entered and quietly closed it behind me. I turned and jumped, Pete was standing off to the side, and I almost collided with him. He steadied me and smiled. "I got here ahead of you. I imagine that's the wedding party lining up and going outside?"

I nodded. "Debbie's down by the stream with Kim Lee; she'll join us soon."

Pete smiled and sat down in one of the chairs. The silence was engulfing, and I lowered my head and stared at the floor. I turned and faced him. "Pete, thank you for officiating the ceremony. Taylor and I appreciate it."

"It's an honour, you are family."

People shuffled in the main hall, instructions were whispered, and I overheard Eddie say "Debbie, no, put that down."

"I guess Debbie's back."

Pete chuckled. "She is a bundle of joy, isn't she?" I nodded in agreement.

There was a light rap on the door, and Pete and I entered the hall. Charity was talking to Debbie and Eddie, then she opened the exit door and peeked outside. I caught a glimpse of guests standing or sitting on both sides of an aisle leading to the podium.

"Debbie," Charity whispered. "You go first, don't forget your basket of flowers."

Debbie nodded and clutched them protectively. The door opened, then she raced down the steps and down the aisle, waving happily to the crowd. When she spotted Mai-Li grandparents, she tried to catch their attention. Charity shook her head, stepped out, and stood on the top step. "Psst...Debbie, throw the flowers in front of you and into the crowd."

Oh oh!

Debbie stopped, turned, and faced Charity. "No, they're my flowers, they're not Carlie's."

The wedding party, guests, and Pete and I laughed. Debbie turned and continued down the aisle; Charity sighed, accepting defeat. Personally, I thought the woman deserved a medal convincing Debbie to march alone through a huge crowd of people.

Charity nodded to Eddie, who was standing quietly to the side, shakenly clutching the ring box. Knowing how shy he was in large crowds, I caught his attention and nodded. He relaxed, moved down the steps and when he arrived at the podium, went and stood next to Debbie, who tried to open the box to find out what was inside. As what only Eddie could do, he whispered to Debbie, and she took his hand and waited quietly.

Charity waved to Pete and me, then left and joined the rest of the wedding party, leaving the door ajar. Pete took my arm; I clutched the bouquet in my left hand. I lifted my head and looked directly at Taylor; he smiled and nodded. My nervousness and anxiety dissipated, and Pete and I walked solemnly down the aisle. When we arrived at the podium, he released my arm, and handed me to Taylor, who eyed me and raised his eyebrows in approval.

Pete turned and faced the crowd. He raised his arms for silence and in a deafening voice shouted. "Who gives this bride away?"

A resounding "WE DO," resonated from the guests.

"I do too," a child's voice shouted.

"Approved by all present and seconded by Debbie," Pete declared.

Laughing and giggling accompanied Pete's announcement, then he raised his arms for silence. The ceremony was culturally diverse, incorporating Canadian, First Nations and Chinese beliefs and traditions.

Taylor and I exchanged vows, then Eddie handed the ring to Taylor, who put it on my finger. Pete smiled and announced, "I now pronounce you man and wife; you may kiss the bride."

Taylor pulled me close, then kissed me, which was followed by an eruption of cheering and shouting. Pete waited for the din to subside, then raised his arms.

"I wish to introduce Mr. and Mrs. Taylor West."

Again, there was cheering and clapping, then Taylor and I turned as one and headed towards Eddie. We pulled him close and hugged him, which started a bombardment of hugs, kisses, and blessings from well-wishers. Eddie reached over and took Debbie's hand; she accepted hugs from both Taylor and me.

I spotted a twinkle in her eye and braced myself. "Carlie," she whispered. "You look beautiful, but you're still not a princess."

Charity and Mai-Li laughed, and I leaned over and said to the little minx. "I know, but you are. Promise me something, don't ever change, okay?"

Debbie grinned and handed me one of the flowers from her basket.

Taylor took my hand, and the wedding party lined up behind us. We walked inside the Hall and headed towards the head table and sat down. When we arranged our wedding, Taylor and I decided not to have a formal meal, instead we opted for a barbecue, which was enthusiastically accepted by the majority. Lance harvested a deer, and there were pheasant, chicken, duck, and fish as well as noodles, vegetables, buns, and numerous side dishes. The food was laid out on a sideboard running the length of the hall, and as we were not sure what the attendance was going to be, extra tables and chairs were set up in the yard. Many of the guests preferred to sit outside on blankets or on the grass.

There was laughter, an occasional howl from a youngster who got separated from a parent, and after the meal, we cut the wedding cake, then Taylor and I danced the first dance. Charity told us the wedding gifts were taken to our place, which we could open later. She warned me there would be a steady stream of visitors arriving at our house afterwards, and if there were any leftovers, to take them home with us. Taylor grinned and looked at Lance, who bobbed his head.

It was obvious something was under foot; I decided it was wise not to pursue the matter.

The noise inside the hall was deafening, and the band, musicians and serious partyers moved outside. The celebration lasted late into the night, those with young children left earlier, and those who lived on homesteads, or were from Princeton, set up tents and camped for the night on the lawn, obviously not daunted by the din. It was decided Eddie would spend the night at Mai-Li's, and Taylor asked him if he was okay with that. Debbie, of course, happily agreed. Eddie nodded, and yawned, and Kim Lee took the two children to the Sih Yuan House.

The music was deafening; people sang and danced. The crowds began to dwindle, and a diminutive number of revellers remained. Taylor leaned over and whispered in my ear. "I imagine this party will go all night; you set to leave?"

"Should we let them know we're going?"

He shook his head, then pulled me behind a tall hedge. "Not a smart idea, unless you are okay having company in your home for the next three days."

I grimaced and shook my head. He grinned, then pulled me around the corner of the Hall and down a winding path. I clung to his hand, trying to keep from tripping over the hem of my dress. The path led to the roadway, and we stayed in the shadows until we arrived at the bridge.

"Keep low and we won't be seen; when we arrive at the Village we'll head towards the barn."

"We're spending our wedding night in a barn?" I whispered.

"Nothing as romantic as that," Taylor grinned. "Lance and I prearranged this days ago, he disappeared from the celebration earlier and saddled Lucy and Thunder, I hid our supplies in one of the stalls. He wasn't gone long enough to be missed."

I chuckled and nodded my head. I must remember to thank Lance when we returned, I had not been looking forward to entertaining a horde of inebriated quests.

The moon was hidden behind a bank of clouds; we moved briskly and soon arrived at the Village. Lance left the barn door ajar, and we slipped quietly inside.

We drifted over to the stalls, and Taylor handed me Thunder's reins, and I stepped back.

"What's the matter?"

"Taylor I still have my wedding dress and shoes on, they'll be ruined."

"They'll be fine until we're sure there's no-one behind us, then we'll stop, and you can change into your hiking clothes."

"Where are we going?"

"Pete offered us his cabin; Eddie was in on it too; he's staying at Mai-Li's until we return."

"Everyone was in on it except me."

"Debbie wasn't."

I sighed, and Taylor lifted me into the saddle. I raised the hem of my dress and tucked it around my knees. "It's not far to Blackburn; we'll arrive there in less than three hours; I won't bother changing my clothes."

Taylor nodded and mounted Lucy, we left the barn, and he leaned over and closed the door. We rode until the Village was out of sight, then Taylor turned on his flashlight. Travel time would have been quicker if we trailed the Similkameen River, bypassing the outskirts of Princeton, using Coalmont Road, except we did not want to attract attention, so we stayed on the Trans-Canada Trail, then turned west into the forest. Taylor knew the back trails, as did the horses, we made sound time, and as anticipated, we arrived in record time in Blakeburn. When we got to the cabin, we dismounted and carried our supplies inside. Taylor lit a propane lantern and took it into the spare bedroom and put it on the dresser.

"I'll take the horses to the corral, don't worry about unpacking, we can do that in the morning."

I rubbed my eyes, and yawned, "I'm so tired I'll be sleeping before my head hits the pillow."

Taylor stopped abruptly and turned to face me. Since I've known him, he was at a loss for words. While he was gone, I dashed into the living room, stacked wood in the fireplace, and lit it, as the cabin was damp and chilly. I returned to the bedroom and washed my face and hands.

I heard Taylor enter the cabin and remove his jacket and boots.

"Are you hungry or thirsty." I called.

"No thanks, I ate enough at that wedding to keep me full for a month," he answered as he moved into the bedroom. He stopped abruptly and smiled.

I was wearing my negligee, waiting for him; he closed the door and approached the bed.

Just to set the record straight, I wasn't sleeping before my head hit the pillow. Good to know!

The End

[If you enjoyed this book, please leave your author a review. Reviews are very important to authors because they help readers find books they will enjoy reading.]

Author's Note

My story is, of course, fictitious, creating a background for my fictional characters. However, I do stress the devastating natural events occurring in my book are not fabricated.

[BWL Author name tag for Shirley Bigelow DeKelver]

Shirley Bigelow DeKelver is the author of six novels: The Trouble with Mandy, Lilacs & Bifocals, Child of the Ancients, and the Climate of Fire Series – Survival, Treachery and The New World, as well as two short published stories, Nature's Precious Gift, and Ziggy's Revenge. She was born in Calgary, Alberta, and after working for over forty years in law firms as an administrator and paralegal, she and her husband Don retired to their cabin at White Lake, British Columbia. She is an avid photographer and many of her photos are published in books and as anthology covers. She enjoys acrylic painting and birdwatching. www.shirleydekelver.com.